PRAISE FOR MORGAN PARKER

NON FRICTION

VOTED #1 "FUNNIEST, SEXIEST BOOK OF 2013"
— GOODREADS.COM

"A funny & real story!! I loved it!"
- *Verna of VernaLovesBooks*

"Read the damn book. It's so good and honestly I could tell you so much more but just find out for yourself. Parker writes amazeballs stories. I have said it before he is a 'smart' writer. One you rarely come across these days… definitely on my Top 10 of 2013!!!"
- *Denise of Flirty and Dirty Book Blog*

"Awesome, a pure joy to read."
- *Martin Skate, author of* The Spike Collection

"Once again Morgan steps over the line and does something quite different"
- *Kelsey Burns of Kelsey's Korner Blog*

"The writing in this book is top notch…. You need to read this book and experience it for yourself."
- *A Risque Affair Book Blog*

"Morgan Parker is one unique author, he put funny, heartwarming, unhappy and sexy all into one book."
- *Jan Kinder of The Pleasure of Reading Today*

TEXTUAL ENCOUNTERS: THE JAKE + CHRISTINE AFFAIR

"A very fast, clever and emotional read!"
- *Leslie Fear, TheIndieBookshelf.com*

"*Textual Encounters* is a prime example of how mind blowing this author is."
- *Nat's Book Nook*

★ ★ ★

non ✭ friction

a novel

MORGAN PARKER

ISBN **978-09917648-2-2**

Follow Morgan Parker on Facebook.

Novels by Morgan Parker:

Hope

Non Friction

<u>Textual Encounters Series</u>

Textual Encounters: The Christine + Jake Affair

Textual Encounters: 2

Coming Soon From Morgan Parker:

Textual Encounters III

Sick Day

PROLOGUE

Our Story

As a child, Oliver Weaver often confused the John Hancock Center with the Sears Tower. It happened mostly with tourists or people unfamiliar with Chicago. Both structures were tall, dark and beautiful, and they were both essential landmarks in one of the country's most impressive cities – Batman Rises and Dark Knight were filmed there, for instance. But that night so many years long after his childhood had faded into a single memory of "everything before Olivia," sitting at a window table of the Signature Room on the ninety-fifth floor of the John Hancock, Oliver Weaver recognized that drawing similarities between two distinct objects of beauty was something he had always done.

While the waitress took Olivia's order, Oliver watched the way his date's lips moved somewhat crookedly when she spoke, the way her long and slender fingers brushed her hair behind her ear to give him an uninterrupted appreciation of her face. He memorized every feature like his life depended on it. And although this woman was not his wife, making a comparison between them was finally something he refused to do.

"The views are amazing up here," Olivia Warren told him once the waitress left. She wore bright red lipstick and a semi-formal dress that he preferred to imagine on the floor of her hotel room rather than draped over her petite figure. "Have you always lived here?"

He admitted to spending his entire life in Chicago – elementary school five miles West from here, a semi-private, faith-based high school in Wilmette, and finally college at Northwestern, followed by his MBA at Kellogg right before his youngest was born. "And you? Has Vegas always been home?"

Their conversation went on in this manner for most of their meal. Innocent and ultimately meaningless, but it meant something- no, it meant everything to Oliver because he knew their time together would end sooner than it should.

When they finished their dessert, they strolled N. Michigan Ave under the lights – walking past Macy's and Burberry as they headed South on the one side of the street, and past the Grand Lux Café, Hershey and the Water Tower as they headed North on the other.

"It's not Vegas," he admitted, holding her hand as they walked, "but it's alive. I always love this part of town after a nice dinner."

Olivia sighed. "I had a wonderful time with you, Oliver."
At the lobby of her hotel, they stopped and stared. They were still holding hands, still smiling from that first moment they truly saw each other. He noticed a glimmer in her eyes that reminded him of the stars or, more appropriately, the lights on N. Michigan Ave a few minutes ago and a single word came to mind: alive. He knew he had the same glow in his own eyes because Olivia made him feel that way: alive.

"I hope to see you again, Oliver," she said.

"You will. I promise." Not soon enough.

They hugged, holding on a little tighter and longer than newly acquainted people normally would, but then again they were more than just two people. When they finally pulled themselves apart, Oliver could tell she didn't want to let go of their time together. He didn't want to let go either.

"Come up to my room?" she suggested.

At that moment, Oliver knew that his decision would do more than just haunt him for the rest of his life – it would forever change it. More than that, it would change him, his personality, his character, everything he ever believed in and loved and cherished.

So when he agreed to accompany this beautiful woman to her hotel room, he knew that some decisions in life are made before you ever have a chance to think them through. And sometimes that's a good thing.

CHAPTER ONE

I always wanted to do something with my life, so when Jennifer decided that our marriage of 12 years, 4 months and 1 ½ weeks just didn't "do it" for her anymore, I figured now was as good a time as any to take that first step. The problem was that if I lacked motivation and direction before her leaving (and I surely did), I didn't even know what those words meant after she left.

As much as I hated her sometimes, I couldn't imagine a moment without her. But I didn't fight her, didn't stop her from packing her shit and all of our daughter's things into our only vehicle

— a minivan that embarrassed me, so I was fine with her taking it just like she had taken the last twelve years of my life — and drove off to some secret place she refused to tell me about. I figured if she wanted to learn the hard way that leaving me was making the biggest mistake of her life, so be it. I could give her a bit of space, no problem.

"Princess, where are you going?" I had asked a dozen times or so on that day, probably way more, but I stopped counting.

"None of your fucking business."

The way Jennifer kept her lips sealed, you'd think she worked for the CIA instead of the local hospital.

I expected her home within a day. After a week, I started to worry. Two weeks, I became a mess. Reality sunk in hard and fast.

And those nights of sunk-in reality sucked. A lot.

I couldn't sleep for more than a few hours at a time; I had chest pains and thought I was going to die; I lost track of what day and month it was. I ached for Princess's body in our bed. And I actually missed Evelyn yelling for someone to cover her up because her blankets had rolled off of her four-year old body in the middle of some dream about whatever it was that kids her age dream about - marshmallows, Barbies, whatever.

Alone in the house, I took the blankets Jennifer had left behind, rolled them up into a body pillow and slept with them.

I called in sick at work. A lot. Sometimes I forgot to make the actual call, which my boss didn't appreciate too much. And in those lonely moments of self-pity, I began to realize that I really needed to dig deep. I had to find motivation and direction, start doing something with my life because that would get me back on track.

And maybe once that happened and Jennifer saw how much better I was, she might even return. Yes, she might move her stuff back, start bitching at me again about all the crap that went wrong in her day. That was what I wanted, more than anything.

So I finally summoned the motivation I needed (to win Jennifer back, to get her and our daughter back into our home) but I didn't know what to do with it. Where do people go with their motivation?

I needed to get laid; that seemed to be the logical place where most newly divorced men my age started. I figured I was no different.

✸ ✸ ✸

It didn't take long for me to learn that the art of meeting women today had changed considerably since my college days; women were Facebooking and Pinteresting, and then there was this strange concept known as text messaging.

I had a lot to learn; I wasn't exactly "tech-savvy." The last time I'd been single, folks didn't send text messages - not unless they had a label maker. And even then, it never got you laid. Not like text messages today.

So after a conversation with Mario, my thirty-something neighbor who seemed to get laid a lot – like so much I used to fantasize about his fuck-buddy-of-the-week showing up at my house by accident - I upgraded my Motorola flip-phone to an iPhone and started taking this texting stuff seriously.

Truth be told, I was hoping Mario could do some of the legwork for me. Instead he recommended a book that he insisted would teach me everything I needed to know about texting women, which was apparently called "sexting."

Despite the promising title and cover, the book was bogus. None of that shit worked. Like at all.

But there was one revelation that came out of *TXT4Sex*. And it was this: any idiot can write a book.

So that was what I did.

Without Jennifer on my ass about everything that ever went wrong, I had plenty of time to write my trashy novel. I decided on fiction because I figured the past 12 years of my marriage had been all make-believe anyway, which meant I had some decent first-hand experience with making shit up.

I started with one word, and then added another and another. Before long I had a sentence, a paragraph, a few chapters even. I was well on my way. And this writing gig really filled the loneliness, it helped me forget how much I missed my family.

And after a few weeks, I ended up with this:

Yes, *Sextual Encounters*. Clever title, right?

Despite *TXT4Sex* being a major waste of $0.99, it gave me all the technical material I needed to write a story about two morons who fell in love via text messages. And sit down because the best part is yet to come (oh yeah, this is abso-fucking-lutely genius).

Being that I hadn't written anything before (not even a grocery list) the idea of writing an actual novel scared the hell out of me. And this was where my genius truly shone because my concept for *Sextual Encounters* meant the story would be told (drum-roll please) entirely in text messages!

Translation: no boring and "deep" narration required!

And because people deliberately fuck up text messages in terms of spelling and grammar, I didn't have to worry about my novel making a whole lot of sense. Without having to use a spell- and grammar-check, that meant I could be a self-published "Indie" author in no time flat!

Yes, I was something of a genius in case you skipped that part.

And the best part of all of this was that women loved authors. Not so much writers (everyone seemed to be a writer these days) or novelists (nobody took novelists seriously because they made stuff up) but *authors* (that was where the real action was).

And that was exactly how I met Emma.

CHAPTER TWO

Needless to say, people absolutely *loved* my novel. They found the romance between Jake and Christine irresistible, which was hilarious because Jake was a douchebag man-whore and Christine was a bit of a, um, runt. There I said it: A runt with a capital C.

Within the first week of my launch, a few heavy-hitting bloggers told everyone about my amazing writing skills, not to mention the unique concept and the "brilliant" (their word, not mine) underlying love story. And holy smokes, *Sextual Encounters* went viral, hitting the Top 100 of Amazon's Romance bestseller list in the first month.

One of my biggest fans was Emma. And let me tell you, she dropped into my life at the best possible moment ever. It had been six months since I last got laid, and all that typing for the novel had left my hands tired and worn out, so the tube of lube and relying on self-service was getting old. Really old.

Then one day, I received her package in the mail. Okay, in hindsight, the fact that she knew my home address should have been a red flag. But I was Mr. Sextual Encounters, the guy that strung a bunch of texts together and called it a novel.

Inside that package was something that made me melt:

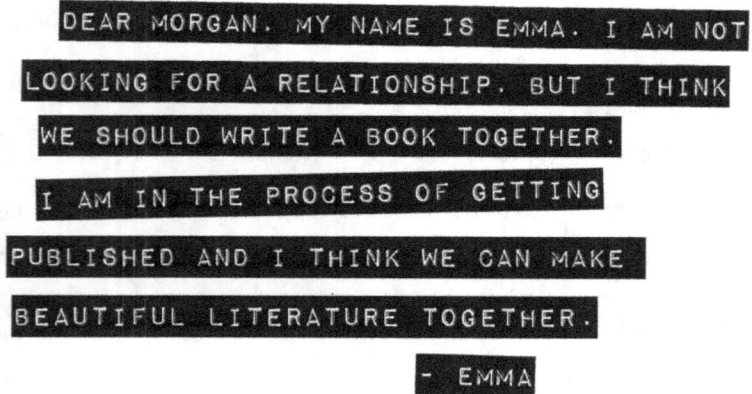

DEAR MORGAN. MY NAME IS EMMA. I AM NOT LOOKING FOR A RELATIONSHIP. BUT I THINK WE SHOULD WRITE A BOOK TOGETHER. I AM IN THE PROCESS OF GETTING PUBLISHED AND I THINK WE CAN MAKE BEAUTIFUL LITERATURE TOGETHER.
- EMMA

No, it wasn't the words so much as the fact that she used an authentic label maker to send me the message. Damn, I felt an instant connection to this woman. But there was something else that made me melt, or at least pushed my body temperature pretty darn high. A pair of lightly worn panties, size petite. They were sexy as hell, and there was a subtle bow that hinted at unwrapping a present that would put a huge fucking smile on my face.

Two months ago, Jennifer had taken our daughter and walked out on me on relatively bad terms, and now I was living like a rock star with fans sending me really hot stuff (only one pair of panties so far, but I knew I'd get more). Anyway, it was the third item in the package that really sealed the deal for Emma and me.

It was a piece of paper with this written on it:

TXT ME @ 212-555-1234

First off, 212 belonged to New York Fucking City. All the big agents were out there and I figured a hottie like Emma knew them all. But I didn't txt her right away. No, I couldn't look too desperate. So I decided to let it go for a few days and that was when my iPhone vibrated. This was what our initial textual encounter looked like:

Emma: Hey there! Haven't heard from you yet!

Me: How did you get this #?

Emma: Did my fan mail scare u?

Me: I don't scare easily.

Emma: That's because you haven't met me yet!

Me: True. But u seem harmless enuf.

Emma: Then come visit me in NYC, big talker!

I should have stayed the fuck away from Emma. She was trouble, right from the start. In the reams of texts that we shared over the course of the following weeks she informed me that she gave birth to her first kid at 18, which was good news to me because it suggested that she liked to fuck – yes, exactly what I wanted. And she had another daughter, a "surprise" pregnancy (which I knew meant "accident"), and that one was the same age as Evelyn. Oh, and she was stuck in a nasty marriage, her second, which was another point on the positive side of the ledger because I wasn't looking to get married. Like ever again. Jennifer sorta ruined all of that romance shit for me, especially by kidnapping my daughter and acting like Houdini all of a sudden.

Because of Emma's marriage, we had to come up with a secret code word, something so clever it made Princess's CIA secrecy look amateurish and infantile. We decided on the code word together, and it wasn't really a word per se. It was more of a symbol and it looked like this:

}i{

We chatted about that symbol at some length. Emma thought it looked like a butterfly, and I agreed with her, but it was more than that. Way more. To me, the image looked more like something I really enjoyed seeing in the nudie pics she sent me. When I shared my interpretation with Emma; she laughed and reluctantly agreed with me, and from that moment on, we texted }i{ whenever we wanted to chat. It was the perfect code word.

And it truly was perfect because Emma's }i{ sure seemed perfect in the pictures too.

⋆ ⋆ ⋆

One Friday night with one hand down my pants and the other on my iPhone (yeah, I was sexting Emma and getting real fucking close because she kept sending me pics of her }i{), my doorbell rang.

I tried to ignore it.

It rang again.

Fuck right off.

The third time, I started to go limp in my hand. I knew it was game over until I dealt with the dickhead on the other side of my front door.

Tucking my junk back into my pants, I left Emma's dirty and flirty text messages on the couch and walked to the front door. And there she was: Princess Bitch. She stood on the front porch, holding Evelyn's hand. I saw the tears in my daughter's eyes and my first thought was that Jennifer wanted to move back in and work things out.

"I think we should consider a shared custody arrangement," she said instead. "I'll come get her on Sunday."

Then she let go of Evelyn's hand, turned and walked away.

✯ ✯ ✯

This shared custody thing would have gone a little smoother with 1) a bit of advanced notice and 2) without getting Evelyn jacked up on sugar one hour before bed time.

And just like how Jennifer wasted the past twelve years of my life with this failure of ours called a marriage, she also fucked up my sexting with Emma. For once, I had to be the one to ignore the }i{ messages as I dealt with the excessive fun of putting my daughter to bed.

Not surprisingly, Evelyn was acting all ADHD about going to sleep, thanks entirely to the sugar overdose. And of course, because I hadn't been able to clear the pipes before Princess Bitch showed up unannounced, I was probably a little on edge myself.

After tucking her into bed for the fortieth time, Evelyn and I started this game we used to play because it was supposed to help her relax and, ultimately, fall asleep.

"You sing a song, then I'll sing one," I said.

"Okay, but mommy says you can't sing."

"And you're not Adele by any stretch of the imagination. But I won't judge you if you don't judge me."

She seemed to accept that.

"So go. You're up, Evelyn."

She sang "You are my sunshine, my only sunshine," and messed up half of the words, but that meant she was finally getting tired so I let it slide and didn't correct her, not even when she mistakenly said "you make me *sappy* when skies are *gay*," instead of "you make me *happy* when skies are *gray*…"

"Your turn, Daddy," she said after releasing a huge, promising yawn.

I started with "Twinkle, twinkle little star," but Evelyn reminded me that she wasn't a baby.

"Something else," she insisted.

"Uh, okay. Any requests?"

"Crazy Kids."

"Which version?"

"Mommy's version in the car."

"Oh, the radio version. I can do that." I started to sing, but when I replaced "fuck" with the radio equivalent, she stopped me.

"No! That's not how it goes!"

Un-fucking-believable. Deep breath, stay calm. "It's time for bed, Evelyn. Close your pretty little eyes and go to sleep." I started to get up.

"Sing!" Okay, the way she screamed at me, she may as well have barked: *Sing, bitch!*

I sat back down, suddenly afraid of this demon child. "Then I pick, and I pick Twinkle, Twinkle."

"No! I'm allergic!"

"You can't be allergic to a song."

"I'm seriously allergic to Twinkle, Twinkle! Something else, Daddy! Now sing!"

I liked the melody of Twinkle, Twinkle, so I went with the closest alternative: the ABC's.

And that was when all hell broke loose. Because in my upbringing and since the start of fucking mankind and probably even time itself, the English alphabet went something- no it went *exactly* like this:

A – B – C – D – E – F – G – H – I – J – K – L – M – N – O – P – Q – R – S – T – U – V – W – X – Y – Z

Yet according to Evelyn – and it didn't matter that I had a healthy 36 more years of living under my belt than she did because I'm the fucking idiot here - "D" comes before "C" and I won't even get started on the notorious "L, M, N, O, P," or in Evelyn-speak, "yellow mellow pee."

Anyway, our first night together ended with Evelyn yelling at me, which hurt more than I let on; I hadn't seen her in almost a month and I felt like she didn't love me anymore. We went to bed angry.

My daughter hated me.

And even I hated me as I stared at the ceiling like a 70-year old geriatric dude unable to get a stiffy to tidy up some unfinished business, no matter how many pics of Emma's }i{ I looked at. All because of some pointless argument with a 4-year old who acted like her mother.

CHAPTER THREE

When Princess Bitch came for Evelyn late Sunday night, she bullied her way into the house and settled at the kitchen table, claiming she was still listed as the rightful, spousal owner on the Deed and until I paid her out she had as much entitlement to the property (and equity) as I did. That pissed me off because I refused to sell the house, but she was right.

"Where did you go?" I asked.

"Fuck you, Morgan. It's none of your business."

I shrugged at her attempted diplomacy. "Something to drink?"

"Fine. I was in Las Vegas with Trina."

I poured her some wine; she was always easier with a bit of a buzz. "Thanks for leaving me with a monster on Friday night."

"Trina hates you, by the way."

"She didn't fall asleep until after midnight, Princess. That's why she's passed out right now and why she barely ate any dinner." I purposely forgot to mention the heavy-duty "anything-you-want" buffet lunch at McDonald's that left Evelyn's face a little green afterwards. Payback is a motherfucker.

"What's this bullshit I'm hearing about a novel, Morgan?"

I couldn't help the smile. "Did you read it?"

"Fuck you, I'm not wasting another minute of my life on you and your bullshit."

"It's pretty good. Got some fan mail already. My next wife mailed me a pair of panties. I'm pretty sure they were clean."

Jennifer drank some wine, but I could hear the gears changing in her head. I could smell smoke, too, which technically wasn't her fault because I was pretty sure her parents were hippies and her mother was still smoking a ton of pot during her pregnancy.

"So, when is my next weekend with Evelyn?"

"I want to do some marriage counseling," she said out of the blue. And then she took another big swig of wine, which really added to the sincerity of her words.

"You still love me, huh?"

She refilled her glass, drank it all in a single gulp, then refilled it again, followed by the same green look that crossed Evelyn's face after our big lunch today.

"What if I say 'no' to the counseling?" I wondered.

"That won't help you if I lawyer-up will it, hun?"

Fuck.

"Tuesday at two." After she drank her third and final glass of wine, she slid me the counselor's business card. Meeting adjourned.

I helped to get Evelyn buckled into her car seat in Jennifer's minivan, marveling at just how simple turning this marriage thing around could be.

★ ★ ★

But then on Monday when I got home from work, I found this handwritten note on my front door:

> Asshole,
>
> Evelyn was ill last night and because you're too much of an idiot to answer your fucking iPhone, I took her to the ER!
>
> McDonald's? Are you on crack? She's FOUR. Don't think this won't get documented!!!

And bring $100 tomorrow for the detailing needed for the van, which still smells like stale puke, thank you very fucking much!

Jennifer

PS - I wish I had never married your pathetic ass

And when I got inside the door, I checked my voicemail and heard this message from Dr. Simms:

"Hey, Morgan. Dr. Simms here. I heard you're a writer and I've got this fantastic and innovative program for creative types like you and your wife. So for tomorrow's session please bring half a dozen photos that inspire happy memories you have with Jennifer. Trust me on this, you'll just love the program! I look forward to meeting you."

Honestly, I was sorta hoping the counseling would get cancelled after the barfing-in-the-minivan incident because Jennifer wasn't one to let water run under the bridge and move on and all of that.

✶ ✶ ✶

The next day at work, Jennifer sent me this email, which crushed any hope of the counseling getting postponed:

A$$hole,

Don't forget we have that appointment today at 2.
And remember the $100.

Jennifer

So I showed up at Dr. Simms' office, a boring and quiet place that reminded me of naptime back in Kindergarten, except instead of New Age music, the office had a receptionist with a fake suntan and a sagging face. This woman had obviously seen more dick ends than weekends in her hard fifty years of living, and it showed in her golden-brown skin.

And then Dr. Simms showed up, stepping out of a room.

"I see you've met my wife," he said. "Jennifer is running a little late, but come on in, Morgan."

We went into his big office with two loveseats facing each other and a glass coffee table between them. There was a desk and bookcase off to a corner.

Just like in the movies, we sat in opposite loveseats, facing each other. It was cozy. Like any good marriage counselor, he asked some conversation-starter questions and informed me that he had been married for twenty-five years. When I told him I was sorry to hear that, the tone of his face changed and he asked me if I understood the importance of marriage in today's "distracted society," and if I appreciated the well-documented impact that broken marriages have on children.

So I asked him if he understood the impossibility of Jennifer and how destructive our marriage was to the sanity of everyone in our household, especially our daughter who still had a fighting chance at being normal, but he didn't have time to respond because Princess Bitch walked in and sometimes actions speak way louder than words, even when those words are coming from a brilliant writer like me.

She apologized for being late but quickly added: "My van smells like McDonald's puke because of this asshole, and I can't stand it."

Dr. Simms frowned. "You can't stand what, Jennifer? The smell or your husband?"

"Both."

And then she sat down next to Dr. Simms.

Hmm. Awkward.

He pointed out that couples normally sit on the same loveseat, you know, for simplicity, but Jennifer refused. When he tried using different words to say the same thing, I suggested we just move forward "as is."

"My feelings aren't hurt," I added for good measure. Then to Jennifer, with a wink: "I'll document this."

After forcing us to produce our half-dozen photos, Dr. Simms explained his theory.

"With creative individuals, I've come up with this experimental therapy where each of you will create a picture book for the other."

"Like a scrapbook?" Jennifer asked, crossing her arms so tight over her chest that it reminded me of how tight she had kept her legs whenever I tried initiating any kind of foreplay. And she did that thing with her eyebrows, like she was better than everyone else in the world. It annoyed me.

"Yes!" Dr. Simms cheered. "A scrapbook is a super idea!"

"I hate scrapbooks," Jennifer clarified, "about as much as I hate Morgan."

"So do I," I chipped in. "The scrapbook part, I mean." The entire exercise sucked big donkey dick, and there was no fucking chance I was going to hang out with Jennifer doing scrapbooking. I couldn't trust her with scissors for one thing.

"Well, at least we have some common ground," Dr. Simms said, shifting a little. The way he spoke reminded me of the music we used to make Evelyn listen to, the Sonia Lee Fisher-Price CDs with enough political-correctness that I always wanted to hug a tree after listening to them.

"It doesn't have to be a scrapbook," Dr. Simms clarified. "Any other ideas?"

I had one: "Can it be a comic book?"

"Of course, Morgan! Brilliant!" Now that was the second time that word (brilliant, in case you missed it) was used by a third-party to describe me. "Anything that incorporates the six photos is simply a super idea. You can start with that, yes!"

I frowned. "No, no, no. I was thinking that Jennifer could do the comic book thing. She's pretty good at graphic design-"

"Fuck you," she barked at me. Mature, right?

"But it's easy," I told her. Like most children, I really *really* wanted to be a comic book hero and I figured this was my only shot at realizing that dream. "Just scan the pictures into Photoshop and add a few speech bubbles and you're done."

Despite her frown, Jennifer's silence told me that she liked the simplicity of my suggestion.

Dr. Simms clapped silently; yes, it seemed he felt we were making progress too. He leaned forward and I thought that if I looked closely, I might see just how excited he really was. But all of that was about to change when he asked: "Now what will you do, Morgan? With your pictures of Jennifer, what medium will you choose?"

Easy. "I was thinking of creating a Ouija board-"

Jennifer had reservations about that. Letting out a bad word, she actually lunged at me, literally flying through the air, across the coffee table and breaking a mug that had been left on it (we would later get billed $25 for the broken coffee mug, which I felt was absolute bullshit because neither Jennifer nor I had been the idiot who left it on the table in the first place, but because it was a Father's Day present from twenty years ago or something, I didn't dispute the charge).

Bottom line: between the $100 to have Princess Bitch's minivan cleaned, the $25 for the shitty father's day cup that *she* broke, and my half of the $350 session, I wondered whether it was not only physically safer but also cheaper to just walk away.

And then there was Emma, who might not have the cleanest record when it came to her failed marriages. But she sent those panties with the bow on them. And she said the sweetest things to me, reminding me that I had a heart, that I deserved to be loved. She was right, too; I deserved it. After staring at her }i{ for as long as I had, I truly believed I deserved it.

So I booked my flight to New York after a big-shot literary agent contacted me and invited me to coffee with him sometime in the near future:

Dear Morgan,

Thank you for the contacting us to discuss your literary ambitions. Your self-published novella, <u>Sextual Encounters</u>, appears interesting and, as you point out, the title is indeed clever. Despite the spelling and grammatical issues with which any traditional publisher might take exception, I would be willing to have coffee with you, at your expense, the next time you are in the New York area.

Kindest Regards,
E. Richard Kindall

Even though he hadn't used official letterhead in his reply, it wasn't too difficult to find his phone number online, but then again it was only the general line for his office. I fully appreciated that once I arrived in New York and made time for him in my busy schedule, I would have to convince his assistants and administrative staff to patch me through to his personal line. But judging by the enthusiasm in his letter (I know, right? I'm a one-way flight away from the big times!) getting that coffee meeting should be a walk in Central Park (yes, pun intended because I'm a real-life author now and I have the fan panties to prove it).

I never understood why so many people bitched and moaned about how difficult it was to build a career as an author. They must be big-time losers because it seemed pretty fucking simple to me.

CHAPTER FOUR

On the weekend, Princess Bitch dropped Evelyn off, again without warning and again with a pickle shoved so far up her ass, she was in her usual, dillish-ous mood (oh, the brilliance keeps shining!).

"Where are you off to this weekend?" I asked.

"None of your business, hun." When she turned to leave, she had a last-second reminder for me: "No McDonald's on Sunday."

I looked down at Evelyn and asked her: "Did you hear Mommy? No fun because it cuts into your mother's life."

"Fuck you, Morgan. You know what I meant and stop using our daughter as your pawn in our problems."

I rolled my eyes then tossed her my fuck-you glare, and as she walked away, I added: "Don't forget your comic book assignment, Jennifer!"

Instead of using her big-girl words, Jennifer resorted to the only sign language she knew – the middle finger.

Once Princess Bitch drove off in the minivan, I knelt down to Evelyn's height and asked: "Have they implemented your recommended changes to the alphabet yet?"

When Evelyn flipped me the wrong finger, I told her: "Wrong one, hun, but you know best! Just like the alphabet."

Sunday night when Princess Bitch came back for Evelyn, there was a glow in her eyes and some natural color in her cheeks. I recognized that look but it had been years since I was the one to put it there.

"You're having sex with someone, aren't you?" I asked. It surprised me that I felt as disappointed about this as I did. After all, Emma was ready, willing and waiting for me in New York next weekend. Plus I was getting to a point where I truly couldn't stand Jennifer because she had walked out on me for no good reason. But yeah, it burned. In a bad way, too.

"And what if I am?" she hissed. "Evelyn, get your stuff and let's go."

"Why?" I asked. I could barely breathe.

"Why *what?*"

"Why everything? Why hurry off and find some random guy? Why bother with this marriage counseling bullshit? Why not just… just…"

She crossed her arms and… and she did that better-than-everyone thing with her eyebrows again. "Very 'brilliant' of you, Mr. Author."

All I could do was walk away.

✷ ✷ ✷

Tuesday at two, I sat across from Dr. Simms and we waited together for Princess Whore to show up. Late again because in her time zone nobody wore watches and they couldn't read the digital clock in their minivans.

He asked me if I had prepared anything for today.

"No, nothing," I said.

This bothered him, as if I had just told him that his wife looked like a washed-up prostitute (which she did, for the record). I fucking hated women. I hated them so much (except Emma, who still managed to find a way to make me smile during this shitty period of my life and Evelyn, who technically was not a woman, not even a lady unless "little lady" counted).

"Morgan," Dr. Simms said in that tone that made me want to break another sentimental piece of shit his kid made for him twenty years ago. "Your marriage will never survive if you don't start taking these exercises seriously."

I leaned forward. "Doc, my marriage is a lost cause."

He raised an eyebrow.

"Yeah. It is. She's fucking some other guy already."

The pitiful look in his eyes led me to believe that his heart might have broken a little for me. But before he could say anything on the matter, Princess Whore strutted in with the same glow on her face that she had flaunted to me this past weekend. For real? Was she seriously late because she was getting laid before our marriage counseling session?

"Did clean-up take a little longer than expected?" I asked.

She sat next to Dr. Simms and smirked, wiping the corners of her lips suggestively. Fucking runt.

"Okie-dokie," Dr. Simms said, leaning forward to provide a bit of a buffer between me and Princess Whore so we couldn't go caveman again and break something else. "Now, let's start with your, uh, 'comic book,' Jennifer."

"Gladly," she said, reaching into her purse and producing something so beautiful it would give the CEO of Marvel Comics a nine-inch erection, maybe even more. She slapped her homework on the glass coffee table like it was that magical exhibit that would win her the court case of the century.

"Holy shit," I whispered, my eyes glued to her comic book cover.

Dr. Simms looked genuinely speechless. His mouth moved, but nothing came out. And I couldn't blame him. This was art, pure fucking art.

"Holy shit," I repeated. "It's… I… Fuck."

Dr. Simms nodded. "Yes. Well…"

Jennifer cleared her throat, and then stared me down. "And what about your shit, Morgan? Let's have a look at that."

I started to speak, but Dr. Simms slapped his hands together and stopped me with a conspiratorial wink. "Let's work with yours this week, Jennifer. We'll get to Morgan's next time."

Jennifer didn't seem to care, and I didn't blame her. Nothing I could write would ever compete with the artistic creation on the table, not a fireworks display straight out of my ass, not the Disney castle made of toothpicks, not the fucking Taj Mahal.

Dr. Simms wiped his hands down his thighs before picking up her pristine comic book by its edges. Like it was gold. Or maybe it looked dirty to him, all of that explicit language.

"Ah," he said, indicating the title.

"It's part of a series," Jennifer added.

"Hmm. Well, let's dig in, shall we?" Dr. Simms said, then opened the book to the first and only page:

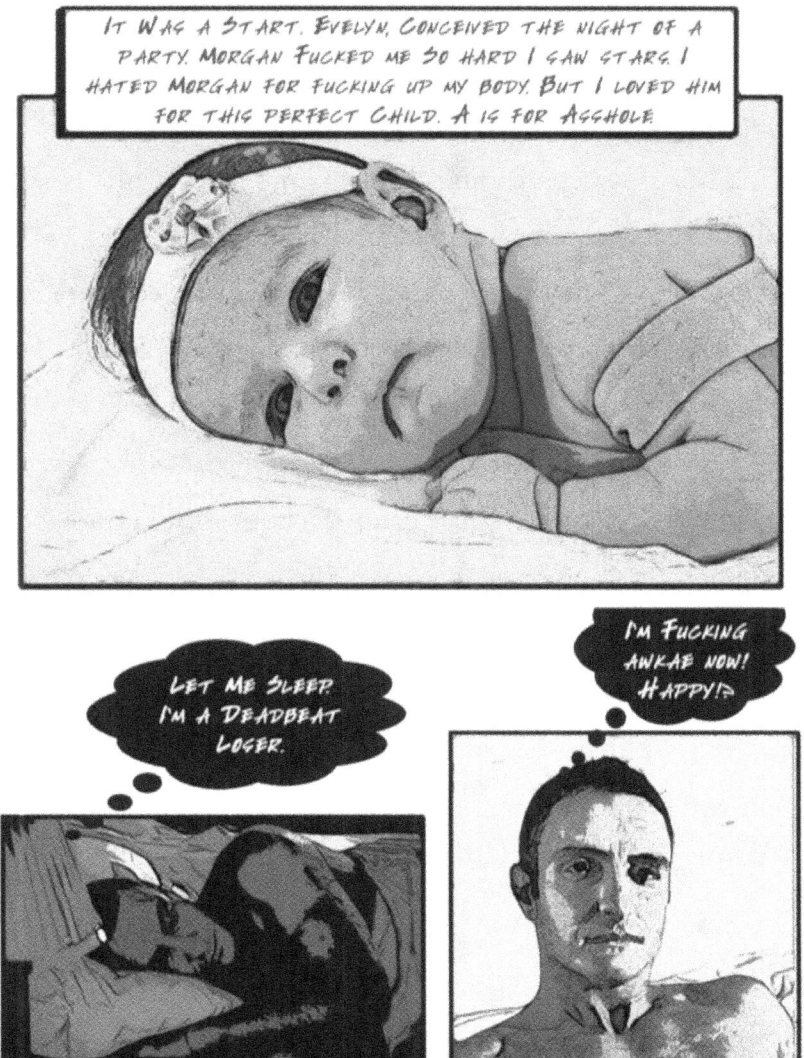

Dr. Simms read the headlines out loud and I could tell by how he said the words more and more quietly that he was not as impressed with the literary content as I was with the graphics and pictures. And yes, Princess Bitch was supposed to use *six* photos of *me*, not two. So I definitely felt a little cheated about that.

When he finished reading, he let out a tired sigh. I was tired too. He looked straight across at me. "Morgan? Are you okay?"

I didn't know what to say. "I… I'm kinda… speechless."

"Yeah," Jennifer barked. "You fucking should be. Because that's exactly you, hun."

Dr. Simms stood up and I thought he might blow a whistle or call for security. "Now, let's just calm the toot down, both of you!" He faced Jennifer. "Jennifer, some of those words weren't exactly, well, complimentary."

She looked away. "It's the truth, Doc. If you want bullshit, go buy yourself a Dr. Seuss book."

"Do you really want this marriage to work, Jennifer?"

"No," I spoke up.

Dr. Simms and Princess Bitch both turned their eyes to me. "Morgan?"

"It's beautiful," I said. "I love what you've done for me, Princess."

Dr. Simms seemed confused, so I elaborated.

"She nailed it," I explained. "I was fucking exhausted when Evelyn came. I remember that."

"Exhausted?" Princess Bitch shouted. "Try absent! Didn't you read the cover, or are you too caught up in the pictures with your third-grade literacy?"

Dr. Simms shushed her. "Jennifer, let's hear him out."

"No wonder you resent me," I admitted.

Jennifer chuckled. "This is a fucking *series*. I'm just getting started. Now let's see your shit!" She flashed her pity-me eyes at Dr. Simms: "This will be priceless, I guarantee you!"

Dr. Simms stood up at that point and announced that our session was coming to an end. "We'll reconvene next week with your homework, Morgan."

I threw my hands up. "Whoa, back the truck up for a minute. You said six pictures, right?"

Dr. Simms nodded and the way he shifted on his feet, I wondered if he needed to go the bathroom or take a hit of Imodium.

"Princess only used two. Her assignment is incomplete."

"Fuck off, Morgan! It's a series! What don't you understand about that? You'll get more, don't get your 'fan panties' in a knot." And with that, she stormed out.

Once she was gone, Dr. Simms let out a heavy sigh. I wondered if we were his worst patients ever; it wouldn't surprise me if we were.

Princess Bitch could be a royal pain in the ass, and our marriage was a complete lost cause. So I couldn't blame him for that look on his face.

"Listen, Morgan," he said. "This isn't going to be easy."

I shrugged, deflated from the emotion of my wife's new relationship and the nitrous pace of her attacks. "But I loved the comic book, Doc. Really loved it."

He handed it to me. "I can't keep this trash here. Take it, it's yours."

I hurried out of the office, afraid of the bill his wife-receptionist was preparing, but I also wanted to catch up with Jennifer. I met her at the minivan, just as she was getting in while texting someone who made her smile, probably the dickhead she was screwing.

"Hey, Jennifer!"

She didn't stop texting. "Hmm?"

"Thanks for this," I said, waving the comic book at her. "It's beautiful. I'm touched."

She stopped texting and shoved her phone into her pocket. "All done?"

I nodded and she got into the minivan without so much as acknowledging me. All I could do was watch her drive out of my life for another week.

CHAPTER FIVE

I loved New York City. After my flight finally found its gate, I grabbed my shit from the overhead and hurried off the plane, one of those assholes that pushes and shoves and gets ahead of everyone else because I'm important. An important and brilliant author.

But all of that effort was wasted because I ended up sitting in the arrivals area with my carry-on in my lap and nothing to do. I texted Emma to see where she was because she had agreed to come get me so we could hang out in my hotel for some much-needed real-life sex. Yes, it had been a few months since we had started sexting and outside of the panties and racy pics she had sent, I really liked her. She truly was perfect with her fake tits, flat tummy, perfect }i{ and flirty promises.

Anyway, I couldn't believe she wasn't there waiting for me, but then again she did have a lot going on with her youngest daughter and something about day surgery for someone else in her family. After a few minutes, she replied that she couldn't make it, so I jumped into a cab and jerked off in my hotel room. Alone.

No biggie, she still met me for dinner.

"Your boobs are way bigger in real-life," I said to her.

"Uh, okay?"

Yes, our real-life relationship started off awkwardly enough, even though I had fucked her at least four dozen times in my imagination. Most people would have expected us to hit it off extremely easily, but we barely hugged outside the hotel at the end of our long dinner.

"Hey, Morgan!" she said as I turned to enter the lobby on my own; we were about to go our separate ways.

"Yeah?"

"I'm really sorry about the airport. Let me make it up to you."

"It's all good, Emma. I promise." I gave her a curt nod, then wandered into the hotel because I thought the conversation was over.

Apparently it wasn't over because Emma followed me inside and grabbed my elbow to stop me from getting to the elevators. She steered me back toward the lobby where we sat down on the stiff hotel furniture that seemed to be constructed of Styrofoam and cardboard.

"Listen," she started, clasping her hands together and stretching her neck like she wanted to get rid of some sudden tension there. "You're a good guy, Morgan. You really are. But I can't do this."

Whoa, was my virtual girlfriend dumping me? How pathetic was that?

Really though, I thought she looked a little worn down in her second wedding ring and those fancy heels and that black dress of hers. This thing about getting dumped by my virtual girlfriend shouldn't hurt like this, but it did. Emma meant a lot to me.

"Morgan? You're so quiet…"

"I just don't know what this all means, where it leaves us."

"I'm sorry." She looked down at her lap, studying her hands like they were inseparable. But then she separated them and placed them on her knees. "But I can do friends."

I gave that some thought and tried to come up with something clever to say, something a brilliant author might spew out and look like a literary hero. "Like pen pals?"

She smiled, nodding. "Yes, like that."

We stared at each other for a bit and the more I looked at her, the more I wanted to hate her like I hated Jennifer. But I couldn't. Emma was everything my wife wasn't. She had not only boosted my ego with those panties she sent me, but she always said the sweetest things when I needed it the most. Plus her boobs were super big in real-life and although that counted for a lot, there was just so much more to Emma. I mean, she had these smile lines around her mouth that promised she'd make an amazingly hot senior citizen, the kind of gal you'd just pray would have her walker break down before siesta time, and you'd have to give her a ride home on your electric scooter. I couldn't hate her if I tried.

Yes, she was *that* perfect.

"Okay. Sure, I can do pen pals."

She gave me a sideways glare as if testing me. "No more nudie pics, though."

"From me or from you?"

She laughed at that. "Neither of us, Morgan. Let's do things right, okay?"

I was a little tired, so I just nodded, stood up and shook her hand, except she pulled me into a tight hug. Despite the pen pals deal and the agreement (unwritten, mind you) to "do things right," I actually got a semi right there in the hotel lobby. It also didn't help that she smelled like lemon cookies, the ones I loved licking the cream out of.

"Morgan…" she said, and by then my dick was rigid hard and ready to go. I confess that I "might" have even rubbed up against her, but in my defense, I tried to be as inconspicuous as possible about that.

"Sorry."

She took a step back, her eyes glowing as she wrestled the look of amusement from her face. "Big plans tomorrow?"

I shrugged. "I'm going to have coffee with that literary agent."

She punched me hard in the shoulder, hurting me and killing what remained of my erection. "Shut *up*! Who is it?"

"E. Richard Kindall."

"Kindall?! Shut the fuck up!" She punched me again, same shoulder. As I tried to rub the pain away, I realized that it was really starting to hurt now.

"Stop that." Then I forced a grin so she wouldn't think she could kick my ass for real, but damn I was tasting pain and doubted that I put forth anything more convincing than a grimace. "Do you like me a little more now that I'm getting signed to an agency?"

"No, not really. But let's have lunch anyway. No, better yet? I'll drive you to and from your meeting. Okay?"

I would have agreed to anything if it meant seeing Emma and possibly dry-humping her again.

CHAPTER SIX

First thing in the morning, I called E. Richard Kindall's office and asked to speak with him directly.

"It's Morgan calling," I added.

"Pardon me?"

"The author of *Sextual Encounters*. He'll know me."

"Please hold."

And so I held. And held. And held. And when the bitchy receptionist returned to the line, she said Mr. Kindall was out of the office.

"It doesn't even take my ex-wife eight and a half minutes to realize someone's out of the office. Let's try a little harder, shall we?" I cleared my throat. "He sent me a letter two weeks ago. Said he'd have coffee with me and now I'm cashing in."

A sigh. "Please hold."

Pretty interesting I was about to be put on hold again when Kindall wasn't even in the fucking office.

"Sir?" the receptionist asked two minutes later.

"Morgan."

"Uh, Morgan?"

"You know I'm here. What's up?"

The receptionist was smirking; I could hear it in her voice. "Mr. Kindall has agreed to see you."

"Who's the asshole now?" I asked, more to myself than the receptionist.

"Pardon me?"

"Uh, nothing. Where am I meeting him?"

Again with the audible smirk: "He will see you at Toshi's at the corner of Broadway and W 26th at eleven."

Wow, I was impressed. In *Sextual Encounters*, Jake and Christine spent time at Toshi's. It was also slated to be the opening setting in *Sextual Encounters Deuce*. This Kindall dude was the real deal.

"Perfect," I said. "I'll see him at eleven."

The line went dead without any further acknowledgement from Kindall's bitch of a receptionist. I made a mental note to mention how poor the customer service was because if I was going to allow him to represent me, I couldn't have a snotty-ass bitch like this receptionist busting my balls each time I called to have a chat with him.

After texting Emma to inform her of when I needed her to pick me up to take me to my meeting, I hopped in the shower and got ready. I created something of an impromptu presentation package that consisted of:

1) An autographed copy of my cover for *Sextual Encounter*s (since it was an e-book, I didn't have real books to hand out, so I settled on this black and white print of my cover art - I couldn't do color because the hotel said its blue ink cartridge was empty).

2) A single-page, double-spaced, two paragraph synopsis for *Sextual Encounters Deuce*, which would be even more successful than the first installment (I had a really good feeling about that, which was a good sign since I didn't have any feelings at all

about *Sextual Encounters* and look at how successful that had been!).

3) A Polaroid of the different fan mail I had received since *Sextual Encounters* was published – most of it from Emma, but I figured he'd be impressed with the panties because everyone wanted to represent a rock star.

4) I wrapped it all in the "Pure Michigan" travel folder I picked up at one of those tourism kiosks in the Detroit Metro airport, which was where I had a lay-over on my way to NYC. In hindsight, I was glad I grabbed it because it lent a certain degree of professionalism to my package for Kindall, and also kept it nice and tidy at the same time.

I was pretty stoked about meeting Mr. Kindall, needless to say. When Emma pulled up in her Vokswagen Golf hatchback, I considered asking her to drop me off a block away. No offense, but I was really hoping she would be driving a Lincoln or Cadillac because it just looked a little weird for someone like me getting into the backseat of a VW Golf.

"Afraid I'm going to bite?" she asked, glancing at me in the rearview mirror.

"Pen pals, remember?"

Her lips rose into a contagious smile.

"Hey, do you think when you pull up to Toshi's, you can get out and open the door for me? Like a real chauffeur?"

Emma laughed, and for a moment, I just stared at her through the rear view mirror, watching the corners of her eyes crease. But she had a viral happiness about her and I absolutely loved it. Eventually, I cracked up along with her, even though I hadn't been fucking around about that chauffeur business.

Despite the fact that she'd found my request humorous, she double-parked next to a Jaguar and got out to open the back door for me when we reached Toshi's.

It was perfect. But what made the moment even more outstanding was the kiss she planted on my cheek before wishing me good luck.

✯ ✯ ✯

Sitting alone at a window table, I watched couples and business people arrive for lunch. Before long, the place was packed. I waited and waited. One particular couple, business associates that smiled and touched each other an awful lot despite the wedding ring on the dude's finger, had ordered their meal, eaten it up and even paid the bill during my wait. I wondered if E. Richard Kindall would even show up.

Of course I knew that it was customary for big-shot agents to arrive a little late, but 27 minutes? That seemed excessive, but that was exactly how long it took before E. Richard Kindall made his appearance. In real-life he looked a lot younger than his website photo. I pegged him at twenty-two in real-life; the web photo had led me to believe he was in his sixties. Then again, Emma's tits had been a lot bigger in real-life too.

Before he could start talking, I handed him the Pure Michigan folder and sat back, crossing my arms and watching him. He looked at it for a good, long moment like he didn't know what to do with it.

"What's this?" he asked.

I reached across the table and opened the folder for him.

A smile curled his lips upwards, and I was starting to feel really good about our meeting. I had great intuition and this was what pro-NBA players might call a "slam dunk."

"Now," I said, rubbing my hands together to harness some of that excitement, "let's see if there's any wiggle room on your commission structure because I'm thinking that your standard 15%

on domestic sales is a little steep when you'll be working with someone like me. What do you say, Rich?"

That moment was what a lot of other authors would consider a "turning point." Because I would soon discover that the E. Richard Kindall sitting before me was not the E. Richard Kindall that owned and operated the big-shot literary agency (now it really started to make a whole heck of a lot of sense why the website picture didn't look anything like the face in front of me).

"Dude, I'm just the intern," the guy said. He closed the folder, rotated it on the table and slid it back to me. I suddenly caught wind of his breath, and it repulsed me almost as much as his condescending tone.

"Oh. So where's Rich?" I asked.

"It's E. Richard Kindall, or Mr. Kindall for everyone except his wife, and *especially* for you."

I felt my face turn a little red, which I tried to stop from happening, but trying only made it worse. "This is unacceptable, a complete insult and waste of my time. If you think I'm going to sign with your fucking excuse of an agency now-"

"Hold on here," the intern said, and his voice was stern. "First off, you can't sign with our agency unless our agency *wants* you to sign. And E. Richard Kindall does *not* want you to sign. Period."

"I…"

"I'm not finished," he said, and his attitude dared me to say another word, *any* word whether it was one syllable or four because he was looking for an excuse to hit me, I could tell. "Second of all, Mr. Kindall sent me because nobody else wanted to waste a minute of their day with a pathetic excuse for a writer like you. They'd rather sit in the bathroom, read through the slush pile, make collection calls, virtually anything else other than sitting here with you."

"I…" I felt hot, constricted, unable to inhale a mouthful of air.

"Still not finished," he growled. "You talked about an insult? Let me tell you, your shitty little self-published novella is an insult to the English language. What have you sold, five copies?"

"Five thousand, two-hundred and sixty-one in the first month alone," I said, but I could hear the cracking in my voice. "That's over ten thousand dollars. Annualized, that's…"

But the intern's laughter stopped me. "Congratulations on the three thousand five hundred dollars you've earned for yourself. You might be a so-called 'bestseller,' but an Amazon bestseller is not the same. Until you're on the New York Times or USA Today lists, or some other big one, you're just a nobody." He stood up at that point, reached into his pocket and produced a twenty-dollar bill, tossing it on the table. "Tell you what, asshole. This is on me, and you can keep the change."

"Thank you," I said, mostly because he couldn't do simple math (five thousand, two-hundred and sixty one copies multiplied by the $1.99 selling price for *Sextual Encounters* was indeed over ten grand, not three thousand five hundred). Plus I didn't know what else to say. I could barely breathe – Jennifer walking out on me hadn't even felt this horrible.

I watched him go, but before texting Emma to come get me, I sat in my seat, took a sloppy sip of water, and focused on some of the breathing exercises I remembered from the prenatal classes from when we were expecting Evelyn.

It didn't help; I was ruined.

CHAPTER SEVEN

Emma knew right away that my meeting hadn't gone well. She got out of the driver's seat to open the back door for me, but I walked right past her and sat in the front passenger seat instead. I felt like dying. The intern's words stung and the only way to describe it was to compare it to a bad case of diarrhea that leaves your ass feeling like it's on fire. Except it wasn't my ass burning into oblivion, it was my soul.

"Hey," she said sympathetically, getting the car moving into traffic. "You okay?"

"I'm great."

"Don't listen to whatever that young prick said to you. You're a *great* writer, Morgan. *Sextual Encounters* was solidly in the top 40 on Amazon for over a week." She gave it a rest. "How many copies have you sold since then, anyway?"

"It doesn't matter."

I felt her hand on my knee. She squeezed it. "When I read your story, I knew right away. You're talented. Truly talented… and that makes people jealous, especially if they didn't have any part in it. He was jealous, that's all."

I stared out my window at the people walking the sidewalk. They were freaks, people who shared nothing in common with me, people in suits who had jobs, places to be, paper to push, false responsibilities that clouded the difference between the important things in life and the really bad things. To them, life was normal, and most of them probably believed it was as perfect as it would ever get in their nine-to-five worlds of bullshit and boredom. Yet they were okay with that. Then again, they weren't writers like I was, they didn't understand. Nobody did.

"Let's go grab some sushi," Emma said, letting go of my knee. "And martinis. That always makes me feel better. Well, the martinis do anyway."

✮ ✮ ✮

After our sushi (I ate) and martinis (she drank – a lot), I ended up driving back to the hotel. Emma said I couldn't drive her home because her husband was there. In her mind, it was more of a hassle to deal with explaining why she had gotten drunk with a guy from out of town than it was for her to spend the night in my hotel room. Good, supportive pen pal friend that I was, I agreed with her that it would be easier to make up some bullshit story tomorrow once she sobered up. When I asked about her kids, she said her oldest was babysitting for the night, at least until her husband made it home.

Translation: I was going to get drunk- and/or pity-laid tonight.

I drove with a hard-on all the way to the hotel while Emma stood through her open sunroof and acted like it was prom night in a Girls Gone Wild video.

I was pretty amped about getting to spend the night with a real, living woman again instead of the rolled up blankets I had been sleeping with lately. The anticipation was so thick and tantalizing that I almost forgot all about my devastating coffee meeting E. Richard Kindall's intern, and I (barely) cared that Jennifer was probably laying on her back right now and staring past her toes while some dickhead made her see stars on his bedroom ceiling.

At the hotel, I left Emma's car with the valet, tipping him $20 because I was about to get laid, then carried Emma up to my room. I kicked open the door while holding her in my arms like it was our honeymoon.

"I'm not fucking you, Morgan."

I didn't believe the words because her eyes told a different story; sure they were closed, but that didn't mean anything. I placed her gently on the bed, made sure her head was cozy on the pillow, then told her I'd be right back.

"Don't leave me," she said. She spoke slowly, the alcohol running thick through her veins by now.

So I cozied up on the bed beside her.

"Hold my hand, Morgan."

I slid my fingers between hers (they fit perfectly), watching her while the alcohol slowly robbed what was arguably my best and only chance at getting laid before flying back home tomorrow.

"My marriage sucks," she slurred.

I ran the back of my fingers along the soft line of her jaw and she seemed to relax a little, seemed to like my gentle touch. "It's marriage, it's not supposed to be perfect. How about we forget about that ring on your finger? Just for tonight?"

Either she didn't hear my suggestion or she ignored it. "That dickhead doesn't know I exist."

"Impossible," I said, then brushed the hair out of her face, tucking it behind her ear. Even half-asleep, fully drunk, Emma's perfection shone through as beautiful as a sunset off the West Coast. "If you were my wife, my days would begin and end with you."

A tear slipped from her eye. I watched it roll down to the pillow and wondered if she had simply fallen asleep.

"These tits were for him. Nothing. I've done photos, racier ones than the nudes I've sent you. Nothing. I've tried everything. Nothing."

I edged in a little closer, my lips about an inch from hers.

"Uh uh," she said, giggling and shaking her head at me. "Already told you, we're doing this right."

"Just a kiss?"

She smiled lazily, turning her head away. "Not a chance."

And just like that, she passed out, her hand going limp in mine.

I'll be real honest here; I considered dry humping her but realized it wasn't worth it. Besides, the coffee meeting came rushing back to me and I lost my appetite anyway.

Fuck.

CHAPTER EIGHT

The next morning, Emma wore big sunglasses that not only covered her bloodshot eyes, but most of her pretty, hung-over face. She looked like hell, even after she showered. And she had barely said anything to me all morning. Still, we had breakfast in the restaurant downstairs, which cost enough to eclipse the GDP of Kazakhstan, and she asked me how the marriage counseling bullshit (she said it) was going. I told her about the comic book and she lowered her glasses and stared straight into my eyes.

"Here's your problem," she said. "Whatever you did to distance yourself from that cunt you call your wife has got her pissed off enough to just walk right out and hook up with some other dude and fuck his brains out. She's probably fucking him right now, Morgan."

"Don't you dare…"

"Yeah, I said it," she spat. "I fucking said it."

I shook my head. "No, I doubt it."

"Don't doubt the truth, Morgan."

I continued to shake my head. "No, not after this week's counseling session. We barely argued and nothing got broken."

"Yes," she insisted. "And she's only doing the marriage counseling to prove that the marriage didn't fucking work so she can convince some judge that you need to give her half of your shit and pay steep support."

"Half of nothing is still nothing."

The glasses went back on and she shook her head. "You should be proud that even your whorish, idiot wife sees that you're a talented and gifted writer."

"Emma…"

"Hear me out. Okay? Because when you think about it, do you really believe she's wasting her design talents on a ridiculous comic book series for you? Seriously, it's not because you're a shitty writer, that's for sure. Not even close."

"Duh, it's because she wants me back," I said.

"Yeah, like she wants chlamydia."

Yes, Emma was starting to piss me off. And all of a sudden I hated myself because while she slept last night, I should have dry-humped her when I had the chance. Better yet, I should have taken pictures with my iPhone of my dick on her face while she lay half-comatose on the hotel room bed. Hindsight was always 20/20, wasn't it?

"Dude," she went on with a tired sigh, "your wife doesn't love you. Probably never did. Now you're her babysitter, and you'll be her support payment once your literary career really takes off. Don't fool yourself. Just because she made you the hero in some stupid 'I Hate My Asshole Husband' comic book series, she does *not* love you, not even enough to live with you."

I took a sip of orange juice, buying myself some time before issuing an official response to her hung-over bullshit nonsense that pissed me the fuck right off.

"You seriously think you're going to save your marriage with this?" she continued. "Your nickname for her is either Princess Bitch or Princess Whore depending on whether you're having a good day or a bad one. That's not love."

"We loved each other once. We'll figure this out."

"How so? Are you going to write her a love story that reprograms her internal wiring from a whore to an obedient, loving wife?"

"Whatever." But the reality was that Emma's last comments sparked my imagination. A love story, huh? It sure seemed I had all the qualifications to pull that one off, so maybe I could "reprogram her internal wiring…."

Regardless, I continued eating my breakfast, in no mood to deal with her pathetic rant about my marriage. At least Jennifer and I were doing the marriage-counseling thing. And as much as I hated to know some other guy was burying his dick inside her, I also acknowledged that Jennifer would eventually snap out of her moment of idiocy; she never would have bothered with that comic book series if our marriage were completely unsalvageable.

"At least we're not living together and pretending," I added between bites, hoping to change directions with our conversation. "We know we're broken, we're trying to fix it."

"Really, huh?"

"Yeah, really. When's the last time your husband even treated you like a roommate? Did he text you last night? Did he even notice you were gone?"

Her dark glasses stared at me, her face so still I wondered whether she was awake. After a bit of silence, I realized maybe I had stepped over the line.

"Listen, Emma, you're a great woman and all that. I'd fuck you in a heartbeat. I don't know what your husband's problem is, if he's fucking blind or gay."

She reached across the table and squeezed my hand. "Thank you."

Her response surprised me because I was aiming for "Retaliation" for all the shit she flung at me about my marriage, not "Empathy." But I nodded my acknowledgement anyway. "My marriage is not the same as yours," I said. "There's hope in mine."

She shook her head and let out a deflated sigh. "No, Morgan. There isn't."

I ignored her. "No disrespect, but I'm not a serial spouse like you are. Neither is Jennifer. If this shit doesn't work between her and I-"

"By 'her' do you mean Princess Bitch or Princess Whore?"

"If it doesn't work, I'm done. Never again."

We played a quick game of stare-down; under normal circumstances I would have won, but Emma was scaring me a little today and since I wasn't sure whether the breakfast (which cost about as much as a mortgage payment) would successfully charge through my Visa account, I figured it was best to eat this meal while it was still warm.

"You'll marry again," she said at last.

"Fuck that."

"We'll see."

✯ ✯ ✯

At the airport, Emma gave me a big hug and didn't let go right away. Like she didn't want me to leave, and that sort of confused me because if she really wanted me here, she would have shown up when I first arrived, and she would have let me fuck her at least once over the past two nights.

When she finally released me, she said: "Good luck with that salvageable marriage of yours, superhero."

"Thanks." I started to turn away, then looked back. I felt a little panicky for some reason. "But maybe you were right about Jennifer. She definitely is a bitch and a whore after everything that's gone on."

Emma shrugged, but I knew she was pretty fucking proud of herself on the inside. "I was out of line. Don't listen to me, just do what's right for you."

I stepped closer to her. "Nobody knows me like you do. I trust your judgment."

She shrugged again, but a smile tickled the edge of her lips. "Go write that stupid story for her. If anyone can win a bitch like her back, it'll be you with your sappy writing. Dork."

We hugged again, and when I started to rub up against her leg, she shoved me back and punched me super-hard in the shoulder. I curled forward, but not because she hurt me (she punched me in the shoulder, not the gut). It was more to cover up my stiffy because sporting wood in the middle of the airport was enough to get the TSA's attention. Which, when you gave it some thought, would be a bit of a boost to the ego if airport security were to label my dick as a weapon of mass destruction.

At least she smiled and shook her head at me. "You're incorrigible."

I nodded. "Yeah. Good luck with that moron husband of yours."

Still smiling, she rolled her eyes and shook her head. "Let me know how that comic book thing turns out."

I stuck my chest out. "I'm a fucking hero, Emma. You slept in the same hotel room as a hero."

"Yeah, uh huh."

I raised my hands like Superman. "Always a happy ending in superhero stories."

"Keep your voice down, dork." She reached up and pulled my arms back to my sides. "My prediction is that this will be a tragedy for you."

I leaned closer and, as requested, kept my voice down. "I doubt it. I know the author."

"Yes and she hates you."

Before letting this conversation turn into a shit-show of massive proportions, I grabbed my luggage and straightened my back. Before walking away, I said: "I'll have her ear for the entire ride from the airport to my house because unlike you, *Princess Bitch* will actually show up at the airport."

"I said I'm sorry."

I chuckled. "I know. But for real, I'll have influence over how this so-called tragedy turns out. And in the end I'll be the hero, the one that always wins."

Emma closed her pretty eyes and I could almost taste her extreme doubt. When she looked at me again, she seemed defeated. "I'll message you tonight so you don't have to fumble through our three-character code word. Safe travels."

"Send me a nudie," I said, then winked and walked away before she could challenge me with the "pen pals" clause.

As I edged through the Security Checkpoint, each step brought me deeper and deeper in doubt about just how confident I should be about my relationship with Jennifer.

CHAPTER NINE

As per usual, I arrived at Dr. Simm's office a little early and since Jennifer couldn't show up to her own dreams on schedule, the extra time allowed me to have a quick chat with our counselor. Just the two of us.

"Did you bring your exercise?" he asked.

I nodded. "Wasn't easy. I was super-pissed when she didn't pick me up at the airport like she agreed to."

He frowned. "How did that make you feel?"

"I just told you: super-pissed. Plus, it cost me fifty bucks to get home."

"Yet you're here."

I nodded.

"Why?"

And that was precisely when Jennifer arrived, a little earlier than she normally would. Maybe she felt guilty about abandoning me at the airport and the conversation that followed where she told me to go find a corner of hell and fucking die.

She looked stunning today, too. She wore a sundress with different colors in it, short enough in the front that you could see how perfectly smooth she kept her legs, but long enough in the back that she didn't look like her regular whorish self. She was still my wife, after all, and I was happy that I hadn't allowed my bitterness about the airport to skew my marriage-counseling homework.

"Sorry I'm late," she said. Wow, that word (sorry) was new to her vocabulary. And I could tell from her tone that she was disappointed about something. At first, I figured she was sorry about sticking me with that fifty-dollar cab ride home. But then the clouds parted and the sun shone through and I realized that maybe this guy she was screwing wasn't as perfect as she originally thought he might be. Maybe there was trouble in Paradise and this was my one opportunity to prove to her that I was the guy she deserved to be with.

"Morgan?" Dr. Simms said.

I snapped out of it and found Jennifer seated next to him, texting away on her phone.

"Are you okay?" he asked, again with that soft "rated-E for Everyone" tone. "I thought we lost you for a second there." He chuckled like that was funny. "Now, we're a little stretched for time, so how about you go ahead and show us what you brought today."

I stood up, stretched my neck, cracked my knuckles and reached into my pocket for The Manuscript.

"You can stay seated if that's more comfortable," Dr. Simms said while Jennifer smiled at something on her phone before tucking it into her purse. Surprisingly enough, she looked up at me, as if she might actually pay attention to what I was about to share.

"It's okay, I'm good," I said, and I could hear the nervousness in my own voice. Fuck. I hated how this was starting out, like the first time Jennifer and I had sex and I was way too drunk and the latex stench of the condom made my dick go limp. It was a freakin' embarrassment of galactic proportions. That was the feeling I struggled with in Dr. Simms' office. I couldn't go limp right then. Figuratively speaking, of course.

"It's okay, Morgan," Jennifer added. "Take your time."

I peeled open the manuscript, which I had folded something like a dozen times so it would fit in my pocket, and with each unfolding motion, I noticed how my fingers trembled. I was being a huge sally about this.

And then, just as I thought I'd die of an anxiety-induced heart attack before I ever finished unfolding the paper, I heard Emma's reassuring voice

"You're a brilliant writer," Emma had said after I shared what I'd written the night before, "an Amazon best-fucking-seller, and this story is better than any shit Nicholas Sparks could ever write, so just relax. She'll cream her panties – assuming that whore wears panties – and when you read it, she'll want the tube-steak sandwich for lunch and the cream-filled dinkie for dessert. Just relax, you got this."

With the pages now open before me, I cleared my throat and began reading.

"Okay, I wrote you a story." Deep breath. "Actually, it's an outline for a story. But I'm going to write this story and populate it with the pictures. I promise." I looked up and neither of them looked very impressed so far.

Shit, it was backfiring, wasn't it?

I steered my eyes back to the page. "So there's this guy, his name's Oliver Weaver and on the same night every year, he goes out to his backyard patio, lights a cigar and smokes it, chasing it down with a bottle of expensive scotch. He does this every year. Why? Well, that's the story." I winked at the page, cursing myself because I was suppose to look up, make eye contact with Jennifer, and give *her* the wink. Shit.

"We flash back in time," I continued, "to find out what brings him to the patio every year. We see that he's married and the marriage is kinda on the rocks, the wife stringing him along and she doesn't appreciate him or give him much room to breathe, much less live

and-"

Jennifer didn't like this. "Fuck you, Morgan! You know that's bullshit!"

Distracted, I looked up, my eyes pleading. "No, it's not us. I promise. Just let me finish."

She rolled her eyes and gave Dr. Simms a disgusted stare. "This is complete fucking bullshit. You know what he's doing, right?"

"Please," I said again.

Dr. Simms nodded. "We still have twenty-three minutes, Jennifer. Let's hear him out."

Jennifer huffed, sitting back in the sofa and crossing her arms. Not happy.

"Okay, where was I… Oh, right. So things are a little shitty, but then he meets someone and her name is Olivia Warren. This Olivia character is flawed beyond anything, can't keep her shit together at all, but she makes him feel super special in a way that his wife never could or would. So they have this quick affair, and she leaves her dickhead husband, but Oliver stays with his undeserving wife who doesn't seem to like him. This pisses Olivia off, see? And so she tells Oliver she's going to start seeing other people to fill the time between now and the time he can finally grow a pair of balls and leave his wife, and she does exactly that."

Jennifer faked a yawn, but I could tell she liked my story. It was her eyes that betrayed her.

"This guy, Oliver, has to make a decision between the woman who has always been there for him, his wife, and this new woman that never escapes his thoughts, not even for a minute of any given day. He's got this wife that doesn't love him like he needs to be loved, but she has never let him down and on paper she meets all of the requirements he needs from a wife. And so he must decide: does he leave this perfect wife "on paper" and hook up with Olivia, a woman who fucks up time and again, who is no good for him at all, and trust that this special way she makes him feel will last a lifetime? What do you do, stay or go?" I allowed the question to linger, hoping they would give it some thought because really, that was *exactly* what Jennifer had decided already – to give up on something constant and real and tested and true and all of that, in favor of some bullshit asshole who made her feel good today but who knows what that relationship might look like in a month, a year from now?

Dr. Simms was the first to speak. "That's very good, Morgan."

"I'm not done yet, Doctor." I looked down at the paper again and found my place. "Long story short, Oliver decides to leave the comfort and security of his long-standing marriage. And true to her promise, Olivia leaves this time-filler piece of shit and agrees to a new life, a life full of love with Oliver. These two people love each more completely than any two people ever could, and each passing day that love only gets stronger and stronger. Except something's wrong, something serious and Olivia, well, she dies. And Oliver is all alone now, wondering what the fuck just rocked his world."

I looked up again and spotted the moisture in Jennifer's eyes. She didn't want Olivia to die because so much had been sacrificed by Oliver for them to be together. And finally, now that these two people could love each other the way they were made to love, it only made sense for a Happily Ever After. Except life rarely unfolded like that and it certainly would not unfold like that in one of *my* brilliant stories, so yes, I allowed Olivia to die.

"That's why every year-"

"On April 4th," Jennifer filled in, leaning closer to see how the story would end.

"Yes, on April 4th, Oliver, who is much older now, sits out on his back patio, and after a few drinks and a cigar that he hopes will kill him real soon, he stares up at the sky." I focused on the ceiling, getting into character really well now. And then I pointed at something imaginary that moved across the ceiling. "And he sees it, the shooting star that tells him she's still there, she's still with him even in death, and she refuses to let go of the love they shared while she was alive."

The Fucking End.

I lowered the paper from my face and found Jennifer's eyes. They were moist and she looked away as she fumbled for her iPhone. I watched her read a text, but no smile surfaced and she didn't bother with a response, at least not at that moment. In fact, when she raised her attention back to me and allowed our eyes to meet, she seemed apologetic.

Well, almost.

And for a brief moment, I allowed myself to believe that maybe this silly exercise that Dr. Simms had prescribed for us would be the pure fucking magic of comic books after all.

CHAPTER TEN

As I walked through the parking lot toward the bus stop, Princess Bitch pulled up in the minivan and stopped next to me. She wore sunglasses that reminded me of Emma's; so big there wasn't much of her face left exposed. No need for sunscreen.

"That was a great story you wrote for me, Morgan. I can't wait to see what happens next week."

Without waiting for a response, she drove off, leaving me standing there for a moment, my body numb from the compliment she had just launched at me. Like a missile. I let it sink in, replaying her words over and over in my head.

That was a great story you wrote for me, Morgan. I can't wait to see what happens next week.

It meant she wanted more. It meant we would see each other next week. It meant I had gotten through to her. At last.

I continued to the bus stop and while I waited I pulled out my phone and texted Emma our symbol:

}i{

Once she replied that it was "safe" to chat, I told her about my success today:

Me: Call me Nick Sparx, bitch.

Emma: It's a good story. I told you that already, dork.

Me: We're gonna survive this.

Emma: You jerk off to my nudie pics. You don't love that bitch.

Me: You're pushing it.

Emma: You're being a tard.

A tard, huh? I'd take that because even if Jennifer and I never saw each other again, at least I had a great story on my hands. A fucking genius story, and Emma was just pissed off and jealous as fuck because it was mine.

I shoved the phone back into my pocket and pulled out the comic book page that Jennifer had created for me last week. The paper was getting worn down, so I was careful to not overdo it. I read only a few words anyway, the ones that really stuck out to me like "loved him."

I had studied this piece of paper intensively over the past week. I did that. I got a little crazy and I knew it was crazy because I never told Emma about the behavior. If it hadn't been so cuckoo, I probably would have said: "Hey, Emma, you know what? I'm always looking at her words. Not just the comic strip, but old anniversary and birthday cards, little notes from when we dated, before we were married, our wedding vows, all of it. I love her words. They're alive. And it's somewhere in those words that I know I'll find the answer to keeping our love alive."

Of course, I would never share that tidbit of information with her. She'd tear my head off for being delusional. And although I understood why she would do that, I also knew that Emma was biased. She wouldn't appreciate that I *knew* Jennifer like nobody else did, on a level that no words in the English language could adequately describe. I knew Jennifer loved me and love like ours doesn't come around every day. There's something special and unique and indestructible about our kind of broken love.

"But every crazy person says that about the person he or she's not ready to let go of," her voice said. In my head of course.

"True. But this is different; Jennifer and I are *different*." My response was also in my head.

"Sounds to me like you're trying to convince yourself." Still in my head.

Seeing how crazy this was getting, I put an end to my internal conversation with a woman who lived in New York City. A woman, I reminded myself, who had promised me another super-sexy nudie pic two days ago… and still hadn't sent it.

CHAPTER ELEVEN

When I got home, I checked the mail and discovered my very first royalty check from Amazon. I wish I could say I wasn't all that excited, but the truth is that when I saw the envelope, an excited yelp escaped my mouth. I wasn't proud of the sound – a neighbor walking his dog had to tighten the grip on his leash.

Once inside the house, I closed the door and pressed my back against it for support. The check could not have come at a better time – Princess Bitch was on my ass about selling the house ever since I quit my day job because my boss had an issue with all of the sick days I had been taking.

And since I had sold over 5,000 copies in my first month, I knew that the $10,000-plus in income could tie me over for a few months and allow me to 1) lease a Porsche and 2) fly Emma up to see how great living out here could be. We'd have fun for a weekend or so, charter a helicopter, rent a boat, and she could help me plot a plan to get Princess Bitch back. That was all I expected in return for the great getaway I would give Emma – her help.

And maybe, if I played my cards right, I might even fuck Emma once and for all. I needed to get laid in a bad way and her fancy pics suggested she'd be willing, despite the "pen pals" bullshit.

Evidently, the anticipation was pretty profound. I tore open the paper and found the check I had been waiting a few months for.

"What the-?" I managed to squeeze out before I lost all ability to breathe. It felt like I had been sucker-punched. The check wasn't for $10K, it wasn't even the $3,500 Kindall's intern said it would be. It was less a little more than $2,700.

Worst of all, I didn't understand what gave Amazon the right to essentially rape me. This barely kept me in my house for two months, forget about those other necessary expenses like, say, food.

Once I managed to recapture my breath, I actually sobbed. I sobbed for a long time, it seemed, a good five minutes or so when I received an email from Emma. I opened the message and found this:

Emma: Hey, handsome. I hope you're having a good day now that you're finished with your marriage counseling with Princess Whore. I'm sure you're not fucking her, so I thought I'd send this overdue nudie pic of your true soulmate – aka me.

I had to hand it to her. Emma seemed to have a sixth sense when it came to putting my broken pieces back together. It always happened at moments like these where I couldn't even think straight; she would manage to distract me long enough to convince me that life wasn't all that bad. Even though my wife was living a new life with some unknown dickwad who was also fucking her (judging by the glow on her face every time I saw her) life was not all that bad.

Deep breath.

Like the pathetic little bitch I was, I wiped the tears off my cheeks and looked at the embarrassing check from Amazon, forgetting about Emma's pic for a minute. I read the small print and discovered that as the writer (i.e. creator of this best-selling, "brilliant" piece of literary genius) I was only entitled to something called "royalties," not the full price as I had wrongfully assumed. In dollar terms, that was just $0.70 of the $1.99 book price. Plus, the IRS held back 30% of that, meaning for every book I sold, I would only ever see $0.39.

I wondered how best-selling writers like Stephen King, Harlan Coben, Danielle Steel and Nick Sparks could survive on such small royalties. How did those colleagues of mine live in such nice mansions? After making the best-seller list, I would be lucky to pay my mortgage and eat for the next two months. I had seen pictures of Stephen King; he wasn't worried about how he would pay for his next meal.

My phone vibrated, and I read Emma's quick text message:

Emma: Dude, are you okay?

I felt the tears starting to burn to the surface again, but just shook my head and wrote a quick response:

Me: I thought BS writers made a lot more than $2.7k/mo.

When she responded, she told me I would probably make bank if I took the story idea I had created for Princess Whore (her words, not mine) and fleshed it into a real novel, not some bullshit cop-out novella like *Sextual Encounters*.

Maybe she had a point. After all, Emma hadn't let me down yet. Ever. Not like the runt I married, who seemed to let me down at every turn.

And I realized that if I ever wanted to repay Emma for her consistent and unquestioned friendship, I had better get working. So I grabbed my shitty little check, and brought it upstairs to my office where I started writing my next novel.

I tentatively titled it *Our Story*.

CHAPTER TWELVE

That night, I hammered out 5,000 words (about 20 pages) of *Our Story*. It rocked so much that when I went to bed at 2am the next morning, I was able to enjoy the full effect that Emma's latest nude picture had on me and within minutes of cleaning up my quick mess, I was sound asleep.

But at eight o'clock the next morning, with less than six hours of sleep in my system, the doorbell rattled me awake. No matter how perfect my writing and pre-sleep "happy time" might have been, dealing with Princess Bitch this early in the morning was the last thing I needed. I took my time getting downstairs and saw her worried, made-up face through the peephole. Although she looked hot in her nurse uniform (or whatever those outfits were called), I could tell by the pent-up rage in her eyes that she didn't want me fucking with her right now.

So I ignored the second chime of the doorbell and, through the peephole, I watched as her face flushed with increased rage. She quickly graduated to livid.

It was hilarious.

In my mind, I started counting and sure enough, Jennifer began to behave as I expected she would; she started pounding on the door with her balled fist in case I hadn't heard the doorbell the first two times.

"Open up, asshole! I know you're in there!" She slammed her fist on the door again and it took all of my self-control to make sure I didn't laugh loud enough for her to hear me on the other side. "I heard your fucking footsteps, Morgan!" More hammering. "Open the fucking door!"

She got a little crazy with the doorbell now, jamming her finger against the button no less than seven times within a two-second span. And at the first sign of sweat on her forehead, I couldn't hold it in anymore. I laughed.

Which wasn't a bright move on my part because she heard me. For some reason during the twelve years we wasted on this mistake called a marriage, she had never heard a single thing I said, not even the most direct comments or questions, but now all of a sudden she heard my chuckling through two inches of solid oak. It was a fucking miracle, a Christmas miracle in the middle of June.

As she leaned her ear closer to the door to investigate my chuckling, I unlocked and opened it so fast that I caught her off guard. I let my eyes inhale her, all of her, and damn she looked good. I quickly understood how I fell in love with her in the first place.

"Jennifer," I breathed, "you look amazing."

She made a face that said "I'm going to puke," and then waved to her minivan, which was parked on the street instead of in the driveway. "Evelyn's sick. She's got a fever and was puking most of the night, so she can't go to the daycare today."

"Is this payback for the McDonald's thing?" I asked, then reached toward her lower back – I needed to touch her, I wanted to feel her – but she turned and slapped my hand so hard that the red sting of her assault glowed on my skin instantly.

"Keep your fucking hands off me, hun," she hissed as Evelyn dragged her sad and sick little body into the house.

"Hi, Daddy, I'm sick," she mumbled.

She stepped out of her shoes and walked deeper into the house.

I heard her settle onto the sofa in front of the television.

"This isn't payback, it's what normal people do and it's called 'parenting,'" Princess Bitch explained. "I can't miss work today, I've been off with her twice since I moved out. As luck would have it, you're unemployed and home doing nothing anyway, so today's your turn to watch over her."

Princess Bitch started to walk away.

"Hey!" I called after her. When she turned around, I added. "We should have lunch sometime."

She grinned, flashing me a sneer worthy of a Breaking Dawn movie, and then returned to the front porch. "Having lunch with you would involve eating. And your face, your voice, your…" she indicated my entire presence, "your… all of you, it disgusts me to the point where I want to vomit." She pivoted on her heels and continued toward the van.

"That's a 'no thank you' I take it?" I asked. And when she refused to respond, I suggested: "Maybe a coffee, then?"

When Princess Bitch reached the driver's side of the van, she threatened me with her pointer finger. "Take care of Evelyn!"

I waved goodbye, gave her my most-pleasant smile and then watched her drive off while she flashed me her favorite finger.

✭ ✭ ✭

I genuinely enjoyed it when Evelyn got sick with the flu. Loved it, in fact. Because during these vulnerable moments, my daughter became something of a Daddy's Girl, which meant cuddling and chatting and, because she was *my* daughter, it also meant confessing her absolute love for me because she felt like she was dying. It was cute, these dramatics of hers.

I refused to assure her that death rarely resulted from everyday influenza because I loved hearing how much she cared for me, how she always remembered, fondly, when I did such and such a thing with her, or how we did this and that together as father and daughter. I melted at her vow to always love me no matter what, so long as she managed to survive this "disease" trying to end her young life (her words, not mine).

Being the good, caring parent that I am, I held her tightly against my chest while also shielding my mouth and nose with my arm so that I wouldn't contract whatever bug her little body wanted to pawn off on me. After all, I couldn't afford to be unemployed <u>and</u> sick.

This was my "quality time" with Evelyn, and we watched television all day long, only taking breaks for her brief sprints to the bathroom to get sick or relieve herself.

"Daddy," she said after a particularly violent trip to the

bathroom. "I might not make it."

I patted the cushion next to me on the sofa. "Come here, Love."

She sat down and I held on to her clammy little hand, making a mental note to use extra hand sanitizer as soon as I finished telling her what I needed to say.

"Evelyn, you know that your father is a best-selling author now, don't you?"

She nodded, her eyes losing a bit of focus. With the fever and possible dehydration, she probably wanted to fall asleep and get some rest. My time with her was short, a commodity I needed to capitalize on.

"Since I'm such a good writer I think you should appoint me to write your biography and as a bonus I'll even script out the funeral service in case you really do die from this."

She asked me what a "biology" was, so I corrected her and helped her get the word right.

"What is that, Daddy?"

So I explained it to her, and then she lifted her clammy little palms to her face and cried into my chest. I shushed her and rubbed her back, listening to the volume of her sobs soften until she finally fell asleep in my lap.

As much as I loved my "cuddling time" with Evelyn, I also

enjoyed my "alone time." I carefully transferred her to the sofa so I could slip away, sanitize my hands and change into a fresh pair pants and a new shirt. I really couldn't get sick; I was not only writing *Our Story*, my next bestseller, but making sure I finished my homework for this week's marriage counseling session with Dr. Simms at the same time. I had way too much on my plate.

CHAPTER THIRTEEN

Princess Bitch called me at six o'clock to tell me Evelyn needed to spend the night at my place; Jennifer claimed she was too busy with an urgent personal matter and she couldn't come to fetch her daughter. Although her cold carelessness didn't really surprise me, it annoyed me for more reasons than one.

First off, after Evelyn's little nap, the Bank called to tell me the mortgage payment was five days past due and they would transfer the account to Foreclosures if I didn't bring the payment up to date within forty-eight hours. So good thing I received my highly discounted check from Amazon, even though I couldn't, in good conscience, drag Evelyn to the bank to make the deposit. And yeah, I couldn't help but wonder how many other bestselling authors were treated this way by their financial institution. Uh, yep, I would be switching *all* of my banking to a private bank once the real checks starting flowing.

Second, Evelyn didn't have any clothes here anymore. The day Princess Bitch decided to walk out on me without any forewarning, she took everything that belonged to either her or Evelyn (except a few blankets). So I was fucked because none of my clothes fit her and as a good parent I couldn't exactly let her sleep in the same clothes she had been slumming around in all day.

Which meant making a trip to Wal-Mart. It wouldn't be easy with a kid who could barely stand up, let alone walk half a block to catch the bus that would take us to the store.

"I don't want to die at Wal-Mart," Evelyn told me from the couch.

"Even if you did, I would never put that in your biography, so don't worry," I consoled her. "Plus, you'll survive."

I checked my watch – it was seven o'clock by now and she didn't even have her shoes on. Yes, I was more than just a little annoyed but I reminded myself that I was the better parent here so I should behave like it. Evelyn needed clothes; she also needed a hot shower because she stunk to hell and back, but without any clothes to change into, there was no point in getting clean.

"Listen," I told her. "We need to get you some new clothes. All females feel better with a new outfit or two."

My words seemed to perk her up a little. She nodded. "I love new clothes." I knew it!

"Once you get into a clean outfit, brush your teeth and rinse with adult-strength Listerine, you'll practically be all better, good as new." And the rest of the world will thank me, too – but I kept *that* thought to myself.

"Yes," she said, and the boost in her energy levels was a pleasant sight. She hopped into her shoes and we were off on our journey to Wal-Mart.

Fortunately, we made it most of the way to the bus stop before Evelyn complained that her legs hurt and she was too weak to carry on the rest of the way.

"Go without me, Daddy."

I considered it, too. After all she *did* stink and I didn't want that stench getting ingrained in my clothes. But I wasn't an idiot. I knew I couldn't leave my daughter on the side of the road for some dog to walk by and confuse her for a fire hydrant.

So I reached down and gave her a piggyback for the rest of the way to the bus stop, allowing her to rest her head on my shoulder. She may have fallen asleep because once we reached the bus shelter and I placed her on the bench, I noticed a bit of drool on my shirt.

"Did you pass out?" I asked.

She denied it, but it wasn't worth the argument, so I let it go.

The bus ride to Wal-Mart was uneventful, which was something I was extremely grateful for. And once we arrived at the store, Evelyn asked if she could sit inside the cart, which was easier than giving her another piggyback, so I lifted her inside and told her not to get sick. She rolled her eyes at me. (That was something some authors might call "foreshadowing.")

"I'm better, remember?"

"No, I said you'd survive. There's a difference." While she hadn't barfed since three o'clock this afternoon, she also hadn't been active, on a bus or in a shopping cart. You could never be too paranoid when it came to vomit.

At the Girls Clothing area, I helped her out of the cart and grabbed a couple of shirts and pants from the Clearance rack to see how they might fit. Once I found the right combination and size, I grabbed a couple more quick outfits, picked some decent underwear, and then packed her back into the cart. If we were quick enough, we might even make the next bus, allowing us to use the transfer slips and save a few bucks on fare.

"Hold on," I said, then made an engine-revving sound before launching into the aisle and racing toward the checkout.

But then it happened: the motion caught up with her and although she warned me with "Uh, Daddy, Daddy, *DADDY!*" it was too late. She hurled all over the clothes we hadn't purchased yet... as well as herself.

Fuck. Cleanup in Aisle Bullshit.

✳ ✳ ✳

By the time I finished getting her cleaned up in the bathroom, I had purchased 2 outfits that went into the garbage, 2 new ones that I would take home with me and 1 more that I changed her into before tossing the old, ruined outfit into the trash. She still stunk so badly that on a multiple choice olfactory test, most people would mistaken her as a dumpster rather than a human child, which meant this new outfit that she wore would also get tossed or incinerated once we made it home. But on a positive note, my gag reflexes had become acclimatized to my daughter's horrible stench.

"Sorry, Daddy," she said, her face so pale I felt guilty for hating her during our little clean-up party in the bathroom.

I leaned forward, kissed her on the forehead, then lifted her up off the floor and carried her to the check out. I no longer cared if I stunk, too – I just wanted to get the fuck out of Wal-Mart and be home and clean.

While we waited for the next cashier, the woman standing behind us - she would technically qualify as a real-life "cougar" - nudged my elbow. When I glanced back, she smiled.

So I smiled in return.

"That's sweet what you did for your daughter," she said. "I saw the whole thing."

I shrugged like this kind of shit happened every day with me. I'm a sweetheart, *grrr*. And then I faced forward, knowing that once Evelyn's stench reached this woman nostrils, our friendly chat would be over. As in dead, like the marriage I was gradually bringing back to life.

"You know," Ms. Cougar went on, "you rarely find fathers who will take as good care of their daughters as you did. That's amazing."

I nodded and smiled at her again, then faced forward. I began a mental countdown to when the rancid aroma of vomit and sweat and sickness would reach this nice-looking woman's surgically enhanced nose.

"But I wonder," this obviously bored-out-of-her-fucking-tree lady went on, "would you have been so attentive if her mother were here with you?"

Okay, that about did it. Calling Princess Bitch a "mother" at a time like this was about as insulting to humankind as nominating Hitler to Sainthood.

"Actually," I said, breathing through my mouth because I *knew* the stench would cut me off if I didn't, "my daughter's biological birth-mother arbitrarily decided to drop her off once she got sick. Now that bitch is at home watching *True Blood* or *Sons of Anarchy* between doing whatever it is that she does with the new man in her life. Because there's no chance she's working on her homework for this week's marriage counseling session. Oh, no. Puke and parenting are two things that bitch doesn't 'do.'"

That put an end to Ms. Cougar's friendliness. And frankly it was about fucking time because the next cashier was available.

✩ ✩ ✩

It was slightly after we stepped through the automatic doors, moments after I paid for more clothes than we left the store with, that Evelyn began sobbing. I leaned down and asked her what was wrong.

She complained that her head and legs hurt.

I stared across the vast parking lot to where the bus stop was located. Damn. It was like staring off the Santa Monica Pier and knowing you had to swim across to Catalina Island.

"I'll carry you," I said, but she didn't even smile.

Evelyn's ungratefulness annoyed me at first, but when I pulled her up into my arms, she rested her head against my shoulder and was asleep by the time I took my first step. She didn't get to sleep for very long, though. A Jaguar XJ snuck up behind us and tooted its horn, startling both of us.

"Hey," came the driver's voice. Aw fuck. It belonged to Ms. Cougar from the checkout line. "Let me give you a lift."

Well, it sure beat carrying Evelyn's dead weight all the way home, so I accepted the woman's kind offer. Once I had Evelyn settled in the backseat, I slipped into the front and thanked Ms. Cougar for her generosity. I offered my hand, but she declined it.

"Sorry. I don't want to catch whatever it is that your daughter's got. But, I'm Rochelle. I'm married and I don't want to fuck you."

I grinned. "I'm Morgan. I'm trying to win my wife back and I'm a best-selling author. I haven't been laid in months and I appreciate your cruel honesty."

She chuckled. "What's the title of your story?"

When I told her the name of my novel, I thought she would have an orgasm right there in her car. She asked for an autographed copy of the book, and when I told her it was only an *e-book*, she looked a little disappointed.

"But tell you what," I said. We were getting close to my street and I knew I had to do *something* for Rochelle, whose luxury car now reeked of vomit after she had probably gone ten miles out of her way to drive us home. "I can print a copy of the cover and sign that for you. Would that work?"

She seemed to consider it, her eyebrows furrowing thoughtfully.

"I'll even print it in *color*," I promised.

Finally, a smile surfaced.

Once we reached the house, I carried Evelyn inside and forced her into the shower to rinse the smell of death off her body. I forbade her from using my Axe body wash because I didn't want to be reminded of this day (ever again) and I knew from this morning's *Good Morning America* that scents trigger memories. I couldn't allow her to stain my memories, so I handed her a sampler of body wash and told her to use that instead.

"Daddy," she said as I was about to leave the bathroom. "This is from Great Wolf Lodge. I'll *never* forget that trip. We had so much fun."

Guilty. Yes, I had scooped the sampler of Great Wolf Lodge body wash — it not only smelled like cotton candy but that weekend had been filled with smiles and happiness and moments I would bring with me to my grave.

"I'll never forget it either, Evelyn," I said, then hurried to my laptop to print off a copy of the *Sextual Encounters* cover I had promised Rochelle.

CHAPTER FOURTEEN

For the first time in the history of mankind, Princess Bitch arrived early for an appointment. Her presence in Dr. Simms' office surprised me, I had to admit. I hadn't seen her minivan outside in the large (but mostly empty) parking lot. And the ex-stripper receptionist hadn't given me a courteous heads up on my way in. Bitch.

"What's going on?" I asked. It crossed my mind that this might be an intervention of some sort, but I didn't quite know what they might be intervening. For the most part, I was fairly well-adjusted, I didn't drink (excessively) or take drugs. I was as clean as they come, I

had six-pack abs and a tongue that made women happy, but then it
dawned on me that perhaps my "problem" was my *writing*.

I knew Princess Bitch wanted me to sell the house so she could
pull her equity out and be done with me forever, but I refused. And
since we were dragging ourselves through this marriage counseling
bullshit at $350/hour at *her* request, she couldn't exactly lawyer up
and convince a judge to force me into selling now could she? I was
snapped back to reality at the sound of Dr. Simms' Fischer-Price
voice.

"… so next week, you and I will have a similar session, Morgan.
Sound fair?"

I shrugged, unsure what he wanted my agreement for – a
colonoscopy, lobotomy, anal sex? Whatev.

"Now, Jennifer," he went on, clasping his hands in his lap and
turning to her. "Were you able to expand upon your comic book
series about Morgan?"

She smiled half-heartedly – it was the first time a grin of any
measure touched those lips since I entered the office, and it occurred
to me that Princess Bitch was distracted. I didn't know why, but I
automatically assumed it had to do with the douchebag she was
fucking. Maybe Trouble had finally made its arrival in Paradise. I
secretly hoped that Trouble was crabs, something superficial and not
permanent or life-threatening because when Jennifer came to her

senses and moved back in, I didn't want to be stuck wearing a rain coat every time we fucked.

"Yes," Princess Bitch moaned. She dug into her purse and pulled out an inter-office envelope from the Hospital. Then she reached inside that envelope and withdrew the latest volume in her "series," and I caught myself sitting on the edge of the sofa, leaning over the table between our two loveseats.

When she placed it on the glass tabletop, I practically died.

"Holy. Shit," I breathed at this week's cover. It was worthy of Picasso's signature. "Can I… Can I touch it?"

I looked to Jennifer first, but she refused to meet my eyes. And then to Dr. Simms, who smiled and gave me an encouraging nod. The paper felt rich against my fingertips and it impressed me that she had gone to the trouble of printing this week's installment in color, which was titled *C is for Cocksucker*. And even though my wife subscribed to our 4-year old daughter's erroneous edition of the alphabet (B, *not* C, comes after A where I come from, and I happen to come from Earth) I didn't bash her effort.

"Wow," I said, running my finger along the art of my face. She had a complimentary way of capturing my strongest features and enhancing them. Like the receding hairline – gone. The scar underneath my jaw – gone. I looked like a beast, and I wondered if this comic-book rendition of me was how Jennifer truly saw me. I raised my attention to her, but she was texting someone on her iPhone and wasn't paying attention.

Maybe this marriage *could* work itself out.

"Let's see what's inside," Dr. Simms said.

I flipped the page to the interior and was slapped in the face with yet another stunning display of Jennifer's graphical prowess:

"Hmm," Dr. Simms said. Judging by the way his rubbed his chin and was frowning at the page, he seemed a little discouraged. Or maybe he was just acting that way because deep down, the graphics got his heart pumping the way it did mine.

Jennifer put her iPhone away and looked up. "Are we done?"

At that, Dr. Simms was a little more elaborate with his *hmm* and he angled his body so that he could face her. "Jennifer, we spoke earlier about what we are doing here, week after week of meeting and working on your marriage."

"I did the homework," she huffed.

I added: "And I love it, too. This is great stuff, Jennifer. I always thought you should have gone into graphic design. You're absolutely talented. I love-"

Dr. Simms rolled his eyes at me and cut me off. "If this marriage isn't something you want to salvage, I suggest we save everyone some time, save you and Morgan a few dollars, and just move on."

Jennifer didn't like the sounds of that. Her face hardened. "We need to fix Morgan. Not just for me, but for himself and the rest of the planet. He will never find happiness if he doesn't learn how to behave and contribute to a relationship. If he thinks-"

"This is *not* entirely his fault, Jennifer," Dr. Simms said, and his Fischer-Price tone matured into something else, something from the likes of Nickelodeon, the "after 8pm" programs. "Just as marital success requires contributions from both spouses, so does marital failure."

She crossed her arms so tightly over her chest that her cleavage swelled into the loose neck of her blouse. I remembered her tits fondly, the way they felt on my lips, their smell, the way I could use them as a thermostat to get her hot or cold.

"So, Jennifer," Dr. Simms carried on, "what do you think you contributed to the failure of your marriage?" He tapped her homework with his finger, forcing my attention from her breasts and back to my comic-book face. "I see a lot of what you think *Morgan* contributed to the failure, but what about you?"

Something shifted in her, something deep and below the surface, such as in her soul, which was a reassuring thought because the jury was still out when it came to whether or not she possessed one of those.

Then Dr. Simms turned his attention to me. "Have you prepared anything for this week's meeting?"

I stood up and reached into my pocket for the folded papers. I had brought only five of the forty pages I had written because I knew it would take at least a year of these sessions to read through all of them. And of course, I had been doubtful about whether we would even get to *Our Story* this week since it was technically Jennifer's turn to present.

"It's okay, Morgan. We won't have time for you today." He turned back to Jennifer. "Remember last week when Morgan read his, uh…"

"Outline," I said, helping him out.

"Yes, remember when he read you his 'Outline?'" He talked about a broken man, Jennifer. A man who misses the love of his life."

"But that wasn't his wife," Jennifer corrected him. "It was a whore he had an affair and fallen in love with. And just to be sure we're all on the same page before you go drawing parallels, the male lead character wasn't *Morgan.*"

Dr. Simms checked the time and sighed. "No, it wasn't the lead character's wife, but that doesn't mean that Morgan doesn't love *you.* It doesn't mean he's not broken."

"I am," I agreed. "I'm broken."

Jennifer smirked at me. "I know."

"Well, folks, that's it for this week. Next week, I want to take a closer look at what you've written, Morgan. And Jennifer, think about your role in the failure of your marriage. Think about your contributions, because until you take ownership, you will never be able to move on."

Move on? What the fuck was he talking about? I thought this was about reconciliation, about helping Princess Bitch see just how fucked up and wrong she was about leaving, and show her that she needed to come back to me.

CHAPTER FIFTEEN

A little numb from Dr. Simms' words – in case he forgot, people generally attend marriage counseling to *save* their marriage, not to be told to throw in the towel because it was time to "move on" – I stepped out of the professional building and started across the parking lot. I had a little more than fifteen minutes before the next bus came, so I wasn't rushing.

And then I saw her. She stood at the mouth of the parking lot, talking on her phone. It seemed she was waiting for someone, which made sense because I hadn't seen the minivan. Maybe she had taken it to the dealership for servicing and had called Trina for a lift.

The details didn't really matter because there she was, and here I was. I could offer my company while she waited, and since our session had gone fairly well, I figured she wouldn't mind standing with me.

The prospect of spending a bit of time with Princess Bitch outside the formality of the counselor's office added speed to my pace, but about halfway to reaching her, a red convertible Porsche turned into the lot and stopped. Princess Whore hurried to the passenger side and let herself in. I watched her kiss the driver, an older man with perfectly coiffed dark hair, a GQ tan that bumped him into another ethnic group and teeth so white that when he smiled, the sun reflected off of them like they were diamonds. He was fucking pretty, no doubt.

I heard Princess Whore laugh – the sound seemed to echo through my world – and then Pretty Boy revved his Porsche's engine and sped toward me so quickly that I skipped between the parked cars just to be safe. As they got closer, Jennifer waved. But it was the look in her eyes that bit me. Those evil eyes, they said something to the tune of "Pretty Boy's tanned dick is gonna be pounding inside me real hard in about fifteen minutes."

I waved back, not nearly as excited about what *I* would be doing in fifteen minutes (sitting on a bus and wondering if it were medically possible to contract an STD from the seats).

But at the last possible moment, Pretty Boy stopped his car right beside me. He said something to Jennifer, so quietly I couldn't hear his words. She laughed at whatever it was, and then leaned on the doorsill, facing me.

"Hey, Morgan," she said. "This is James. He wants to know if we can give you a ride home." Then, because Pretty Boy Jim couldn't see her face, she glared at me and mutely said "no."

I didn't want an argument. I also didn't want to see just how perfect he really was – I could see all that well enough from here, in fact. And yes, he was pretty, the kind of guy you'd want your daughter to marry, the kind of guy you wish would have taken your daughter to Wal-Mart a few days ago so she could have puked all over him instead of you.

Although I couldn't exactly breathe, I forced a fake happiness onto my face and shook my head. "No," was all I said. "No."

"Perfect!" Princess Whore replied, then faced forward and said, "Let's go, James!"

Except Jim didn't "let's go." He leaned forward, one hand dangling over the steering wheel and the other draped over the shifter, his fingers touching my wife's bare knee. "You sure, dude?"

he asked. "I don't want any hard feelings here. Let's keep this as unawkward as possible. You know, for Evelyn's sake."

First off, unawkward wasn't a fucking word unless Evelyn had made up her own fucking Webster's Dictionary now that she had invented her own alphabet. Second off, his fingers were on my wife's knee. It was bad enough I had to ride the bus home; I wasn't going to let Pretty Boy Jim take pity on me and drive me home before he fucked my wife. No way. I may as well suck his dick.

I tried for a full-face, 100-watt smile, but realized I was lucky if I pulled off the half-face version. "Yeah. I'm sure. Thanks for the offer." And then I started walking again, not wanting to look at the red Porsche that cost more than my house or the vanity license plate I didn't want to memorize (GR8DAY).

What kind of douchebag puts a vanity plate like that on the car he drives someone else's wife around in? It baffled me that he could be *that* much of an asshole.

Fucker.

And even though my own father's name was James, I fucking *hated* that name now. Absolutely loathed it.

Whatever happened to "Bros before Hos?" Wasn't that supposed to be the unspoken oath among men? You *never* fuck a married woman. Jim needed to… he needed to fucking *die* for what he had done to me and my marriage.

Before I could start plotting Pretty Boy's death, my phone vibrated. I saw the text message from Emma.

}i{

I replied back with a simple: What?

> Emma: U OK? Haven't heard from you in 28 hours and 43 minutes... I miss U. Hit me up when UR free <3

Yes, Emma possessed a magical skill for making me smile. Once I reached the bus shelter, I texted her back.

> Me: I met PW's new BF

> Emma: Is he hot?

> Me: Fuck you.

> Emma: I detect a bit of resentment.

> Me: Yes. He's VERY hot.

> Emma: You need to move here.

> Me: Can't. Not until Evelyn's 18.

Emma: LOL. Why 18?

Me: She'll be an adult then. Not my problem anymore.

Emma: For such a brilliant guy, you're an idiot sometimes. She's UR daughter. She'll always be your problem.

Me: Fuck you X 2.

Emma: Move here and maybe U can ;-)

Me: You're such a tease.

Emma: U <3 Me.

Me: Sometimes, yes.

When she didn't respond, I tucked my phone into my pocket and pulled out Princess Whore's comic strip – *C is for Cocksucker* – as the bus arrived. I paid my fare with nickels and dimes, then settled into a bench for two, right in front of the rear doors, and kept to the aisle so nobody would bug me while I read the words of Jennifer's art.

And like all of the things she had written for me, I looked for something to find strength in. I saw:

"*… made for the big time…*"

and

"*…time to walk…*"

Those two lines made me realize that if Princess Whore had fallen in love with me once, she could certainly fall in love with me again. She wasn't throwing in the towel with lines like those. There was no doubt in my mind that I could win her back. No doubt at all. None.

I finally admitted, right there on the city bus that smelled of an old drunk, that maybe I had been a little depressed after Evelyn was born. Having been married for more than half a dozen years and not having to share my wife had been something I had clearly taken for granted. But then Evelyn arrived and Jennifer had to split her time between me and this whiny little shit who needed constant attention. And of course there were the *physical* changes that happened to women after they pushed an 8-lb human being through their, well, you know…

Before I could think too much about my contribution to the failure of our marriage, my phone vibrated in my pocket. I pulled it out and saw that Emma had finally responded.

> Emma: I'm coming to C U this weekend. Need to get U out of UR funk.

The thought of entertaining Emma made me smile real big. Like the 100-watt, stupid big that failed me in the parking lot a few minutes ago. I texted back right away.

> Me: Can't wait. And I'll even show up at the airport to pick U up.

> Emma: Shut up, dork! You don't even have a car!

She had raised a good point, but my second month's royalty check was due any day now, and it would be a few thousand dollars, a little less than the one I received for the first month. If I timed things just right, I could afford to let next month's mortgage payment go a little late and pay down my credit card instead. And with the newly available credit, I could rent something from Hertz for the weekend. Yes, that would work. I texted back.

Me: I'll have a car for you. Don't worry. And you'll love it, it's bigger than your VW.

Emma: Shut up. I'll be happy as long as when I leave, you're happy that I came.

Me: Depends whether you come all weekend, or just the day you leave.

Emma: Perv. Gotta run.

I tucked the phone back and realized that while I had been busy using some of my *Sextual Encounters* material on Emma, I completely missed my bus stop. I was two stops out of bounds.

Shit.

I snapped the bell cord, disappointed (but not entirely surprised) that a woman had distracted me from the important things in life.

CHAPTER SIXTEEN

When I saw Emma coming toward me at the Arrivals gate, I felt like Special Agent Dave Kujan from *The Usual Suspects* as the truth rushed to him in a wild montage of images – the poster on the cork board, the name of the China company underneath his broken coffee cup, and so on. Except instead of truth, the images that rushed to me were the nude pics that Emma had continued sending to me in spite of her own warning that pen pals didn't send those kinds of things to each other. I never argued with her, though.

And she looked way more beautiful in my hometown than she had in New York City. Stunning, really.

"You're beautiful," I said, giving her a hug and breathing in her lemon-cream filling smell. Again, like last time, I wanted to lick it right out from her.

When she eased out of my embrace, she eyed me suspiciously. "You look like shit, Morgan. What's going on?"

Ignoring her question, I gave a sideways nod toward the airport's parking garage and we both chuckled before heading off in that direction. Even though I had never picked Emma up before, we had talked about our trek to that parking garage. How I would pin her up against my car, which I would have parked in some far-off, hidden corner, and then lift her skirt and go down on her. That would not happen today, though; she wore a pair of white pants that stole away the possibilities of oral pleasure in the parkade. Plus, the pen pals thing and her claimed desire to "do things right" sorta fucked up my hopes too. I still didn't know what that meant, but I had no desire to push it. At least not here in the airport.

Once we reached the car, which I had parked in a far-off, hidden corner, Emma's jaw dropped. She had a *what-the-fuck* look on her face.

"It's a Porsche," I said. "Just like Pretty Boy Jim's."

"Except Pretty Boy Jim's comes with Princess Whore."

I opened the door for her and placed her luggage in the back seat. "The way I see it," I explained as I struggled with the ignition because it was to the left of the steering column instead of the right, "that motherfucker is renting my wife. I'm renting the car. Just like the car goes back to its rightful owner, Princess will come back to me. So it all balances out."

Emma rolled her eyes and said nothing else. She was likely just as impressed with the Porsche as I was.

We were halfway home when she asked me why I was driving at the speed limit. So I told her: I could barely afford to rent the car, forget paying a speeding ticket. She chuckled and called me crazy, then told me to "punch it."

"Huh?"

"Put the cock to 'er," she said with a Fargo-ish accent, and then braced herself in the seat.

Still a little confused by her ghetto talk, I put both hands on the wheel because I thought maybe she wanted me to drive a little more prudently.

Emma laughed and the sound was infectious, as beautiful as listening to Vivaldi's Four Seasons live at Carnegie Hall (well, as beautiful as I imagined it would be). "I'll pay the speeding ticket, dork! Just *drive*."

I pressed my foot to the floor and the Porsche responded with a purr I could only describe as… erotically addictive. It inspired greed – I wanted to keep pushing the limits, and I wanted more. A lot more.

All of a sudden, it made sense why dickheads like Pretty Boy Jim couldn't be happy with an awesome car, why he broke the Bro Code and wanted to fuck my wife. With Emma beside me, I wanted to fuck her too. In truth, I had always wanted to fuck her, even before I was greedy like this, but the Porsche made that greed come alive.

When I pulled into my driveway, she said my house was "cute."

"Until I'm getting paid like a bestseller, it's all I can own," I admitted.

"I love it! For real!" She grabbed her bag and walked to the front door, waiting for me to let her in.

"You can sleep in Evelyn's room if you're okay with that, or you can you sleep in mine." I opened the front door and we walked inside.

"Will you be there?"

"Uh, yeah. It's *my* bed."

She shook her head. "Then I'll take your daughter's room."

I headed upstairs with Emma on my heels. She commented on the family photos on the stairwell wall, the color of the second floor landing, the carpet's thick under-padding, the layout, how clean my house was (yes, I spent all day yesterday tidying up and figuring out how to turn the vacuum cleaner on). I chalked up her chatter to nervousness.

"Here's Evelyn's room." I pushed the door open and waved her inside.

"I can't sleep in that," she said, pointing to the Barbie-racecar toddler bed.

I shrugged. "Then I guess you'll have to cuddle up next to me in mine."

Emma laughed.

Of course I had known that my daughter's toddler bed would be too small for Emma to sleep in, but I didn't exactly think she could fault me for wanting to get her in bed with me. After all, she was still sending me nude pics and sometimes our texts became so flirtatious I swore I could feel her breathing against my neck.

Besides, it wasn't like I was telling her that she had to shower with me in the interest of saving water. (Although depending on how the rest of our afternoon unraveled, I might just take a swing at that suggestion before the day ended).

"Okay, fine. I'll sleep in your bed."

I suppressed my grin, happy with her quick decision. I reached forward to give her a hug and maybe get the mood started with another leg rub, but she dropped her bags on the bed and left the room before I got too close to her, effectively slamming the door to romance in my face.

"Now let's talk about business," she said, obviously playing hard-to-get. I followed her downstairs into the kitchen and watched her open my refrigerator, grab a bottle of spring water for herself and offer me something to drink.

"I'm good," I answered, taking a seat at the kitchen table.

She sat across from me and drank straight from the bottle, devouring half of it in a single long swallow. She asked me about the sales trends for *Sextual Encounters*, and I answered that they were starting to taper off, decreasing slightly on a week-over-week basis but nothing so serious that I would have to go find a real job anytime soon.

"You need to promote the book a little more than you are," she said like she worked for CSI: Amazon.com. She definitely spoke with great authority, though. I trusted her words, trusted her ability, and I knew that if I listened to her I might just be able to make a bit more money. "Do you have a pen and paper?"

I hurried to the clutter drawer and found some paper and a pen with *Dr. Simms – Marriage Counseling* printed on the shaft. Although I didn't want to appear too eager and desperate, I knew that my quickness was obvious.

"First off, you can start increasing your revenues by bumping your sales price. I know it sounds weird, but your sales are still fairly strong – you're in the Top 100 as of seven this morning. So I suggest bumping it to $2.99 and if it completely kills your sales, then go back to your $1.99 price point. If sales stay strong, consider going to $3.99. Monitor it closely for the next few days and adjust the price accordingly."

It humbled me that Emma had stalked my sales rank this morning before getting on her plane; I promised myself to be gentle with her tonight in bed, maybe start off with some mild spooning, a few funny jokes and a neck massage. Yes, a neck massage for sure.

"Second, you need to create some social-media buzz." She wrote down an elaborate plan that would allow me to interact with my fans on websites like Facebook, Twitter, Pinterest, all of the usual suspects. "And third, you need to start showing your face at author events."

I asked what those were, and Emma said she had attended several as a fan and would definitely make a presence as an author, as often as humanly possible. Apparently, these events were similar to flea markets for authors where a bunch of us set up tables or booths in a hotel conference room. Like a wedding show. Hordes of fans would flock to the event for my autograph, ask for sneak peeks into my next story, chat with me and so on. It was a way to meet people and get the fans really excited about my work, and Emma said that if I did it properly, my fans would promote my book to all of their friends and family, so it became viral, increasing exponentially like a bad case of strep throat.

"So it's like a real-life book signing," I said, "except on steroids because there are other writers there and it's more of a, well, an event."

"Yes," she said, happy that I understood. The way she explained the dinners, parties and socializing, not to mention that most of the people who showed up were women looking for a good love story… it all sounded like a blast. But then she gave me the biggest benefit of all:

"You can align your events with mine," she said. "So we can be together more often."

Huh. I hadn't even thought of that. "That's a, um, super idea."

Our eyes locked and I knew she could read the images flashing across my mind – running back to the hotel room for some wild sex while the other authors whispered behind our backs about our hot and steamy love affair; holding hands underneath the large dining table during those group dinners; leaving the author parties early and hanging out at the pool long after it closed for the night; stuff like that.

"Alright, that was easy," she said, pulling her gaze away. "I'll be at the Washington Romance Authors Event in a couple of months promoting the release of my book. It'll be published by then. And *Sextual Encounters* will fit right in."

"Sign me up. I can pre-promote the release of *Our Story*." And then I had a stomach-dropping thought: "How much will all of this cost?"

She ran through a laundry list of costs — the booth, the room, the flight, the promotional materials like banners and bookmarks, the dinners and other activities. "I'd budget for a couple thousand dollars."

Maybe she saw the color drain from my face. Or maybe I made a noise and blacked out for a minute because the next thing I knew, she was standing over me with her big fake boobs in my face.

"Maybe you shouldn't have rented that Porsche for the weekend, huh?" she asked, chuckling.

"I thought women like Porsches."

She didn't really find that funny, so she returned to her side of the table to get back on track. But I could tell something bothered her.

After staring down at the notes for a few minutes, she looked up and there was something in her eyes.

"You know, Morgan..." she started, and I had an "uh-oh, here it comes" feeling as she prepared the rest of her statement in her head. "There's a reason Princess Whore isn't here right now."

"I know," I admitted. "She's confused, angry. She's working through things, trying to figure it all out. But eventually she'll see that nobody can love her as perfectly as I do. And that's when she'll come back."

Emma heaved a deep breath like I just broke her heart. And maybe I did, maybe that explained why she decided to trade up from Evelyn's toddler bed and sleep next to me despite the risk of being dry-humped in the middle of the night. "What if she doesn't come back?" She let that question sink in for a bit.

"But she will," I countered.

"It was a 'what if' question. What if she doesn't come back?"

I thought about it. "Then why would she bother with the marriage counseling?" I asked. "Or shared custody? And really, she hasn't pushed all that hard for me to sell the house. If she never intends on coming back, the marriage counseling would be over, she'd fight for full custody and the house would have been listed by now." I felt my cheeks burning, like I was pissed off or offended when I really wasn't. "And the comic book, Emma. I'm not saying I'm perfect either. But twelve years... I mean, that's got to count for something."

"It counts for a comic book?" she asked, still staring absently off into the distance.

There was something in her eyes that told me she couldn't believe she had heard the words that just dropped out of my mouth, but then she simply shook her head and got back to the business of the Washington Romance Authors Event.

CHAPTER SEVENTEEN

After spending a couple more hours planning for my first author's event, Emma said she was hungry and I knew what that meant – time to get changed and look for a place to eat. Since renting the Porsche had cut into my budget by a fairly large margin, I knew it would have to be someplace relatively cheap. We wouldn't be hitting the trendiest bar or restaurant, that was for sure. So we headed upstairs together and when I started getting undressed in my bedroom she asked me what the fuck I was doing. So I told her.

"This is where I'm getting changed," she said. "And you need to get out."

"But it's my bedroom," I protested.

"I'm your guest. If you prefer, I can stay at a hotel." She waited and of course I kept my mouth shut because I didn't want her staying at a hotel. I wanted her to stay here, in my house, in my room, in my bed. With me.

"Fine. I'll use the office." So I grabbed the clothes I wanted to wear to dinner and retreated to the office where I changed into them. I was surprised by Emma's reluctance to change in front of me and, quite frankly, I didn't understand it at all since I had already seen so many naked photos of her. It wasn't like I would get a peek at something new. Not even close.

Regardless, once we were both fully clothed, we met downstairs and I told her she looked stunning. She wore black pants and a blue top, her face freshly touched up with some makeup she didn't even need, and it still didn't register with me that maybe Emma was the closest thing to perfection that I would ever meet.

We left the house in silence and for no other reason than I wanted to see her smile, I opened the Porsche's passenger door for her and before lowering the convertible top, I asked if it was okay.

"Might get your hair all messed up," I explained.

She said it was fine and driving those five miles to the Olive Garden made me wonder why I didn't get on the Interstate and take her to the next town. There was an Olive Garden there too, and it would have meant more time in the Porsche with her. I really wanted to get the engine purring again – she seemed to like that – and I knew that once we sat down at the restaurant, things could get awkward when we had no other distractions to fill the silence if our forced conversation encountered them. And I didn't want to talk about Princess Bitch because it seemed to bother Emma more than it bothered me. Like she was jealous, even though she was technically married and wouldn't fuck me anyway because we were pen pals doing things right.

At the restaurant, we were seated in a quiet booth and I ordered the house wine because there was a special tonight where you'd get a free dessert and 10% off your entrée if you purchased a bottle.

"So?" she asked after the waitress poured our glasses. "Tell me more about this story you're writing. What happens next?"

That softened me up a little, so I told her. "It starts with the male lead character – I called him Oliver - stepping out to the patio late at night and firing up a cigar. He drinks his single malt, breathes in the fumes from his cigar while silently praying that he dies. Like right there, right then, the best thing that could happen to him is death. And while he prays, he stares at the sky and that's when he sees the shooting star. It happens every year on this 'anniversary.' And he knows it's her, speaking to him from the grave. So he smiles, and we cut to when he meets this dead woman years prior."

Emma chuckled. "You said 'cut to' like it's a movie."

I nodded. "That's because I'm a visual author. So it very much feels like a movie. A short, good movie. Not a long and boring novel."

It seemed to me that she thought I was joking, but I meant what I said. If I wanted to differentiate myself from other romance writers, I needed to produce a movie-quality story in the form of a book. For example, anyone would rather watch *The English Patient* five times back-to-back than read through a single chapter of the book. Even *The Notebook* seemed more entertaining as a movie than a novel. I knew all of that, so right from the start, I thought of *Our Story* as a movie in the format of a book, not as a long book that would have readers wishing for self-inflicted illiteracy so they could just go out and rent the DVD.

"So, how does Oliver meet this 'other' woman?" she asked.

"On an airplane. She's a writer and he's an accountant, which is what I took in school because I hated the idea of having to write an essay. Anyway, they both hate flying and they hit it off. When the plane lands, she invites him to her book signing the following day."

"Oh, like an Author Event."

"Yes, exactly, except it's just Olivia – that's her name – and not a bunch of her competitors crammed into a conference room with her. Anyway, after the signing they hang out for the day. Oliver calls in sick and he takes her to see the city. And they fall even deeper in love. Except it's a forbidden love because they're both married."

"Do they... ?"

"No," I answered, shaking my head and realizing that I hadn't eaten enough today to be drinking this much wine. I cut myself off – I couldn't leave the rented Porsche at the Olive Garden overnight. "They don't have sex. And after their weekend together, she gets back on her plane and he goes back home to a shit storm of bullshit because he missed his ten-year wedding anniversary while hanging out with this other woman that he obviously didn't fuck, but nobody believes that so he starts thinking maybe he should have."

Emma laughed. "Sounds like New York."

"Actually, it's Chicago," I said, correcting her. I would realize later that night that what Emma really meant to say was that my story reminded her of our time together in New York, specifically that day when I met E. Richard Kindall's unkind intern and Emma got drunk. Ah, yes, New York, where I had the opportunity to dry-hump her while she lay passed out in my hotel room bed, but I didn't. "When Olivia goes back to her husband in Las Vegas, she ends up breaking up with him. It's a sad relationship, he's a complete asshole. Emotionally abusive and he doesn't really pay much attention to her except to fuck her and have someone do the housework for him."

"Jeez." She shifted in her seat and I wondered if she knew that in a lot of ways Olivia was based on her.

"I know, it sounds a lot like your marriage. Except it's not," I lied. Because Olivia doesn't have the baggage of all of those kids to carry around with her."

She rolled her eyes and called me a douchebag because two kids was the norm, and then she took a long pull from her wine, long enough to finish her glass and refill it. Her hunger for the alcohol reminded me of the time Princess Bitch came to my house and said she wanted to do the marriage-counseling thing – three glasses of wine in a little more than three minutes. I tried not to think too much about Princess Bitch, though. I focused on the story, on Emma instead.

"So now Olivia is ready to pursue this relationship with Oliver. Yes, it's long-distance, yes it's a little inconvenient, but when all you've got is distance between you and your soulmate, that's not a bad thing, right? Distance is something you can control; meeting your soulmate in the short span of a lifetime is something you can't."

She smiled at that and gave an affirmative nod. "I say, 'Act on the things you can control; don't worry about the things you can't.'"

I snapped my fingers at her, grabbed my iPhone and fired up the Notes app. "Exactly. I need to write that one down." While I finger-typed the quote, Emma watched me, her eyes taking in my excitement and passion for this story, for *Our Story*. It wasn't even close to *Sextual Encounters*; this one was a real love story, a forbidden and difficult love story that spanned decades, a lifetime (well, for one of them, anyway).

"So then what?" she asked as I tucked the phone away.

"Well, Olivia gets pissed off. She's willing to take action. In her eyes, she already has. She left her husband and now it's time to wait. Wait for Oliver to leave his wife so they can decide where to live – in Chicago or Las Vegas."

"Let me guess," Emma said. "Oliver doesn't leave his wife."

Our meals arrived and I took a couple of big bites to get some food in my stomach and soak up the alcohol. I couldn't believe the effect of the wine already – I didn't even remember ordering the meal, I had been buzzed and rambling about *Our Story* too much to remember.

"He should," I added. "Oliver should have left her because he obviously doesn't love her and she doesn't love him, but he's committed to his vows."

"He was playing 'Sick Day' with another woman on his tenth-anniversary!"

"I know, right?" I shook my head, grinning. "But he sticks it out. And his wife doesn't want to let go either. She's stubborn. They both are. They have kids and they want to preserve the marriage for the benefit of their kids. Always the fucking kids," I half-mumbled because as much as Olivia was based on Emma, so was Oliver.

"That doesn't make sense," Emma said. She poured more wine, she had barely touched her food. This subject clearly annoyed her. "It's worse for the kids to live in a dysfunctional home filled with anger and hatred."

"Try telling that to my marriage counselor," I sighed.

"And what's Olivia doing this entire time?" she asked. At last, she bit into her pasta.

"Olivia gets confused because she thought Oliver loved her and would do anything for her, but to Olivia, he's picking his kids and, worse, his wife over her. Really, he isn't. He's determined that he won't end his marriage because of another woman, so now he's just waiting for his kids to get old enough. In his mind, once they're off to college he intends on packing up and moving out."

Emma semi-shrugged. I could see she was buying into Oliver's rationale, maybe because she recognized herself and her own logic in his actions. I didn't want Emma to think I condoned Oliver's reluctance to end his marriage, so I shifted gears a little.

"But Olivia starts to get a little angry and impatient. Because ten years is a long time, and that's how long it will be before Oliver's youngest is off to college. So she calls Oliver one night in tears and dumps him."

"But he's her soulmate," Emma argued.

"So? He's also married. And Olivia hooks up with someone else, an internet guru with tons of money and a big dick, which is way more exciting and lucrative than an accountant with a kid. He's got a Porsche, too."

"Ah, he's Pretty Boy Jim!"

I grinned. "Guilty. Except the big dick part." Why did I have to say that part about the big dick? "But Oliver doesn't like that. He sees his years of hard work, of working on distancing himself from his non-present wife, of preparing for the day that his youngest goes off to school slipping through his fingers. All he has ever wanted was Olivia. And even though he was hesitant to believe it at first, he truly buys into the reality that Olivia is his true soulmate. He sees her fading into the history books of ex-girlfriends, so he starts to panic."

"Does Olivia fall in love with this Pretty Boy Jim guy?" Emma asked, really interested in the story now. Probably, she had too much to drink on an empty stomach, just like I had. "She can't fall in love with him, Morgan. Not if Oliver is her true soulmate."

I sighed, ate a little because I honestly hadn't written half of what I just blurted out. The story was just dropping out of my mouth, words that I would probably forget by the time we got home and cuddled up in bed tonight. Damn, I knew I should be writing this stuff down. It was the type of material that all of my reviewers and bloggers called "brilliant" (again, their words not mine).

She reached across the table and smacked my shoulder. "Tell me she doesn't fall in love with him!" A few people at other tables snapped their attention at us, the two young people who drove to the Olive Garden in a Porsche who were drinking too much wine because it came with a free dessert.

"Okay, okay. She *thinks* she falls in love with him."

"Bullshit. How can you 'think' you love someone? Morgan, this story sucks."

"No, wait. She thinks she loves him because he's there to fill the time. A time-filler. And because she can't have Oliver, she doesn't know any better. It makes sense because Olivia's looking at the relationship in front of her, comparing it to waiting, and wondering if she'll die alone if she keeps holding out for Oliver to show up. And so far, he hasn't left his wife, even after she left her dickhead husband. Do you understand now? It's easy to think you love someone when the person you really want isn't there for you, at least not physically." Damn, this was starting to hit a little close to home, it sounded way too obvious, even to my own biased ears. I changed gears again before stuffing bread into my mouth. "And really, Olivia's version of Pretty Boy Jim isn't that bad. He's kind of a good guy actually."

She seemed to think about the story while eating more of her meal, and I used this pause to indulge in a bite or two as well.

"When Olivia stops responding to Oliver, when she ignores him for a year or so, Oliver gets on a plane and flies to Vegas. He just goes to her because he can't stand not having her in his life. He wants to take her by the shoulders and make sure she looks into his eyes and sees straight into his soul when he tells her just how much he loves her. And while he's plotting his script on the plane, he also plans on kissing her and he believes it will be that kiss alone that will satisfy her for the rest of their days apart. He's sure of this because he's so sure of their love. In fact, he has never been so sure of anything else."

"Wow," Emma said, half-mocking me. "Nothing else?"

"Nothing."

"Not even that she's too busy being 'in love' with Pretty Boy?"

"Shut up. Oliver didn't think that far ahead."

"Clearly," Emma added, rolling her eyes. "So what happens when he shows up?"

I wanted to tell her – the movie was playing on the screen of my imagination, but I had to put it on Pause because the waitress came for our mostly empty plates and asked if we wanted dessert. Emma passed, which disappointed me because dessert was free with our bottle of wine, but I didn't put up a fuss. I realized that maybe Emma just wanted to get back to my place and do the cuddling thing in bed.

"So?" she asked once the waitress left. "Oliver shows up in Vegas and…"

"And that's when he sees something he didn't expect."

Emma leaned forward on the table, her Bambi-eyes as wide as a full moon. "What!? Tell me!"

"Calm the fuck down," I said, maybe a little too loudly because the someone in the next booth seemed to choke on her food and a man in another booth said, "That just about does it!" but no one ever said anything to us.

Emma grimaced and whispered: "Tell me!"

So I leaned forward onto the table as well, but before I could tell her, the waitress arrived with our check and asked for us to pay immediately.

It seemed we had become something of a distraction to the other patrons at the Olive Garden. Already we were better suited to the New York lifestyle.

CHAPTER EIGHTEEN

After parting ways with the Olive Garden (I swore I heard a cheer erupt behind us once we stepped out of the restaurant) Emma begged me to take her to a Baskin Robbins for some mint-chocolate-chip ice cream on a sugar cone with sprinkles. I didn't know what the hell that meant, but I knew where there was a Baskin Robbins, so I simply steered the Porsche in that direction and bought her whatever it was that would put a happiness on her face. It was worth it.

"Don't drip on the seats," I warned when we returned to the car.

"It's a rental."

"I need the deposit reimbursed so I can make next month's mortgage payment," I explained.

That seemed to settle it.

After the ice-cream stop, we ended up at the "Overlook," which was a look-out at the side of the highway that peered down at the water. Since it was starting to get dark, the view was pretty romantic. The sky was starting to turn and because of the partial clouds, there were blues and purples and pinks.

"You don't see this kind of thing in New York City," she said as she unbuckled her seatbelt and stepped out of the Porsche. I didn't want to leave the car, but I wanted to follow her, so I did.

We stood at the wooden railing and looked… somewhere. It wasn't so much the view that I loved so much as I enjoyed just being there with her, this close in this romantic setting. It was the togetherness; I could smell her and feel her and while she licked at her cone, I realized something that I really didn't want to realize.

"You're quiet," she said with a voice that would normally set the stage for a perfect first kiss. "Are you okay?"

I let out a pensive sigh, the kind that only brilliant authors can get away with, then snuggled into her a little. She knew what I was trying to do, she wasn't an idiot, and when she chuckled at my attempt I knew there was no chance her tongue would transfer from licking the ice cream to licking my face.

"I'm not going to fuck this up," she said, staring out at the water or pretty sky or something else that you could only see at the Overlook. "I'm married. You're still married, at least on paper. I'm doing things right, Morgan."

Ugh, not *this* lecture again. "I respect that. Because once you give yourself to me, I want it to be special. I want it to be 'right' just like you do."

She kept licking her cone, maybe to hide the subtle smile from surfacing. "You're trying to save your marriage, Mr. Big Talker. You think I'm going to listen to your bullshit?"

"Oh, I'm not saying I *want* us to hook up." What I wanted was to fuck her, to see what a twice-married, mother-in-college woman was like in the sack. Like going to the rodeo – you never really wanted to be a cowboy, but with enough beer in your system, you sure wanted to take one of those bulls for a ride. And if I kept telling myself that, I figured I would believe it. Every single word of it.

"You're such a romantic," she said, chuckling. "Then what is it you want from this penpalship of ours?"

"I think sometimes the stars align whether we want them to or not. And we're drawn to certain people and places for no other reason than… Destiny."

She liked that. After all, I was the bestselling romance author and maple syrup sappiness was supposed to be my specialty. I snuggled in a few more inches. If I kept this up, she would be giving me a piggyback before the sun disappeared over the horizon.

"Destiny, huh?" she said. "So far you've got *A is for Asshole, C is for Cocksucker*, and now *D is for Destiny*?"

Her prediction for the title of Jennifer's next installment made me laugh, hard. If I had been the one licking the ice cream cone, I would have choked on it and possibly died.

CHAPTER NINETEEN

I woke up the next morning with a sore back from sleeping on the sofa in the "office." It was a pullout sofa, but I refused to open it up, too afraid of finding one of Evelyn's uneaten meals from her infant days crusted in the folds. Plus, I remembered that the mattress sagged so badly that if I ever did fall asleep, I would have sunk below sea level.

And I only slept in the office because Emma told me at the last possible minute that I could not sleep in my own bed if she were there. She kept saying that she wanted to "do things right," and I didn't understand it at all – I thought she had agreed that we would sleep together. After she shot down my heads-to-toes suggestion, I tried kicking her out of the room, promising her she was petite enough that Evelyn's toddler bed would not be terribly uncomfortable, but as my guest she won the argument.

This morning, I was the first one downstairs, so I made eggs, toast and bacon. I hoped the smell would rouse her from her sleep so she could see how much pain I was in, but she slept in. Her eggs started to discolor and harden, but I left them on the table anyway. The only reason she woke up at all was that the doorbell rang.

I worried that it would be Princess Bitch looking to drop Evelyn off, whining that something else had come up with Pretty Boy Jim. But when I opened the door, it turned out to be a little worse in some ways.

"Rochelle," I breathed. I was surprised that she remembered where I lived, she had only driven me home that one time. From Wal-Mart. "Wow, what brings you out here?"

She handed me a little card. "Sandy and I are having a small get-together tonight. We were driving through and I thought of inviting you."

I was speechless as I accepted the invitation, glancing out onto the street and finding her husband, Sandy, sitting in a yellow, convertible Corvette. He gave me a head nod and a trendy wave and maybe even a wink behind his aviator glasses, but I couldn't be sure about that.

"So?" she asked. "We'll see you tonight?"

Then, from behind me in a voice so scruffy it would give a male country singer a hard-on: "Who's that? Princess Whore?"

Rochelle's face blanched. "Oh, I'm sorry. Are you and your wife...?"

I shook my head. "No, it's not what it looks like." I faced Emma: "Good morning, sunshine." And then I closed the door, stepping onto the porch with Rochelle. "She's a friend."

She raised her eyebrows, curious.

"A non-fucking fuck-friend, I guess. A non-friction friend. Lots of pics, lots of flirting, but no action." I shrugged. "Either I'm doing something wrong or my face is wrong."

"Or she's in a relationship," Rochelle said.

"Something like that." I didn't want to go into the details of Emma's marriage – they weren't my details to share and I didn't want to look like a home-wrecker – so I nodded at Sandy again (he was actually a good-looking dude and judging by the sunglasses, tan and the way his chest hair peeked out over the top of his unbuttoned shirt collar, I figured he worked for one of the high-tech companies in town) and told Rochelle I would show up even though I was skeptical about bringing Emma out in public after her recent display of antisocial skills.

"Perfect," Rochelle said, her smile beaming again. Then she turned and headed back down the front walkway to the flashy Vette.

"Nice car," Sandy called out to me as Rochelle eased into the passenger seat. Sandy had been referring to the Porsche in my driveway; I wasn't in a hurry to tell him it was a rental. He revved the engine, then drove off with a casual wave and I was immediately impressed with Rochelle's husband. He was the kind of classy guy I wish Jennifer had hooked up with, not that Pretty Boy geriatric fuck. But then again, I doubted someone of Sandy's caliber would even look at my greedy, narcissistic wife…

I walked back inside and discovered Emma hunched over the kitchen table, chomping an apple.

"I made you some eggs," I said.

"They're not eggs anymore. They're shit."

I stared at her, my face burning up. I wondered why she had to be so fucking hard on me this morning. Having forfeited my bed for her and even making breakfast despite being exhausted, was it wrong to expect a bit of gratitude?

"So who the fuck was that at the door so early in the morning? She woke me up."

"It's ten o'clock, and it was Rochelle. She's a friend. Very loyal."

"She's the cougar from Wal-Mart."

"Yes. And she's married and she's sweet and she's done more for me during the three weeks that I've known her than you've done for me."

Emma chuckled. "I'm sure she has."

I gave it some thought, wondering whether I detected a bit of playful jealousy. I decided to pursue that angle. "Yes, actually. She has."

"So you're fucking her," Emma stated, studying the apple in her hand briefly before turning her attention back to me. "Because that's the *only* thing I haven't done for you, Morgan."

I rolled my eyes to see if she would bite and give me a more-definitive cue as to whether she truly was jealous, or just being a pain in the ass because she obviously wasn't a morning person.

"What did she want so bright and early on a Saturday morning?"

"She's having a party tonight and wanted me to come along. Probably because she knows that Jennifer hasn't been treating me well. And after your PMS-ish behavior, she probably thinks I've got a thing for being emotionally abused."

"Huh." She walked over to me and put on her pretty girl smile. I almost expected her to bat her eyes. It was cute and although I gave no indication of it, I really enjoyed Emma's change in attitude. "So what are we bringing to this party?"

✶ ✶ ✶

We spent the day shopping. Well, I spent the day shopping while Emma had her hair styled, her fingers painted and had something else done to her feet, something that looked like it would hurt and tickle at the same time. In all likelihood, I would have kicked the young spa girl in the face if she did that to me, but once it was all said and done, Emma actually looked relaxed. Even her feet looked good.

When she asked me what I bought for tonight, I opened my Target bags and showed her the chips – all flavors of the rainbow – and the box of wine, which was highly discounted because the expiry date was tomorrow, but would still fill something like 40 glasses.

According to Emma, I was an idiot and the stuff I bought wasn't good enough. She made me return these items for an in-store credit ("Buy your daughter a new bed," she suggested). We found a boutique vintner where she forced me to buy a dessert wine that cost more than all of the other items I had just returned, as well as a chocolate treat that was ¼ the size of a real chocolate bar and had a name on it that didn't belong to Hershey; it cost as much as the boxed wine, the pre-mark-down price.

When I pointed out to Emma that there was barely enough

chocolate here for one person to enjoy, she said it would be nice for Rochelle and her flamboyant husband to end their night with the wine and treat themselves to the rich chocolate before fucking.

"You don't seriously think that will work, do you?"

She nodded, convinced. "Of course it will."

"Then I should get some for us."

She shook her head at me, called me a dork, and said she needed to go buy herself an outfit for the party. "I didn't pack for this."

Rochelle and Sandy owned one of those homes on a street that you would drive to see how the other 2% live. Their McMansion was of two-story variety, with a driveway that cost more than my entire neighborhood and was large enough to accommodate six families. There were floodlights too, and they showcased the stone exterior. A black iron fence tidied it all up and as Emma and I headed up the front stairs, I wondered if that fence were electrified.

Someone in a tuxedo welcomed us into the lobby (it was bigger than a traditional foyer) and pointed us past the music and food and pretty people to an outdoor oasis that made me wonder if this place was our town's version of the Playboy Mansion. The backyard had everything short of a Ferris wheel.

After I grabbed two champagne flutes (I handed one to Emma), Rochelle intercepted us and bumped me into Sandy's small social group. Before I could object, Rochelle took Emma by the hand and introduced her to her own entourage on the other side of the awesomely cool swimming pool.

"She'll be fine," one of the men said, and I relaxed.

I formally introduced myself to Sandy and thanked him for having such a sweet and thoughtful wife.

Inevitably, as Sandy's friends flocked to other groups or left for drink refills or hors d'oeuvres, my conversation with Sandy turned to my writing and I started to tell him about my latest story, the one that was supposed to save my marriage and bring Princess Bitch back to me. Sandy smiled politely and nodded like a good host, but just as I was distracted by watching Emma carry on an animated conversation with a group of Rochelle's friends (it was actually impossible to *not* notice Emma in that elegant dress of hers and her freshly painted fingernails and new shoes that added a few inches to her height) Sandy was obviously distracted as well. But a guy like Sandy was always distracted; with this big house, a Vette for the weekends and a wife that stayed home full-time, he had a lot to deal with. So I came right out and dropped the bomb.

"What do you do, Sandy?" I asked because 1) I was curious and 2) my book failed to capture his attention.

He told me he was an accountant by trade and the CFO of a tech company in the city. Bingo!

"Funny, I went to school for Accounting," I admitted.

"Yet you're a writer?" he seemed half-amused by this. "You make stuff up."

I shrugged. "I enjoyed the program. I never had to write an essay." He chuckled at that and nodded at the fond memories. "Plus, there's something satisfying about the way every entry has its place. How you can solve problems by getting to know the origin of each number. And, of course the cliché: I just love how everything is in balance when the books are done properly."

"Amen." Sandy raised his cup. We clanged our glasses and drank a little more than we should have. His eyes wandered to Rochelle (what kind of a top was she wearing, anyway – it covered the front but left her back completely exposed) and my own eyes quietly found Emma sitting at the ledge of the swimming pool, the long back of her dress pulled aside while her legs dangled in the water. She was alone and looked beautiful, unaware as I admired how the light that caught the rim of her hoop earrings, the soft wading motion of her feet in the water, the far-off look of loss on her pretty face.

Sandy patted me on the shoulder, snapping me back to reality. "If you ever decide on returning to the corporate world, let me know, Morgan. We're always looking for smart accountants."

His offer was touching but corporate culture believed in something called structure and showing up every day, on time. Not to mention all of the other bullshit that I didn't have to deal with as a best-selling indie author. I smiled politely and thanked him for the offer. "I'll keep that in mind," I added.

And now it was my time to leave, abandoning him in favor of Emma, my own guest who had come all the way from NYC. I kicked off my shoes and sat next to her, rolling up my pants to my knees and letting my feet dip into the water.

"Nice place," Emma said. Her voice had slowed down and quieted, and it brought me back to that moment where I watched her from the other side of the pool. Emma always looked great, but right now she was the most beautiful woman alive.

"Nice everything," I said, watching the pretty crowd. Everyone appeared to have been plucked from the latest set of *The Bachelor*. Smiles and nods all around, gorgeous on tap.

"It'd be real nice to be set up like this," she said, and she looked at me. I felt like her words were challenging me.

She was right, it would be real nice. While you couldn't bring these material objects with you when you died, I was always told that life was more about the journey than the destination, and owning really cool shit sure made life's journey a lot more enjoyable.

I checked my watch because it was probably at this same time yesterday that Emma made me realize a little something I hadn't been looking for. Last night, it had happened at the Overlook. Tonight, the realization was that those feelings could belong to me permanently.

"I'm not ready to leave," she said.

"Neither am I. Last night at this time, we were watching the sky turn colors." When I glanced over at her, I watched the memory curl her lips upwards. I wondered why her husband was such an asshole, why he never noticed these beautiful little things about her.

"Rochelle seems like a really nice person." She shook her head as if a little embarrassed. "I can't believe I was a little jealous of her this morning."

"*D is for Destiny*. I don't know how I would have survived the bus with my barf-stinking daughter if Rochelle hadn't shown up and offered us a ride."

My attention wandered across the beautiful crowd and I caught Rochelle and Sandy off in a corner, cozy and talking. I admired how perfectly matched they seemed to be, and I started to wonder about my own, personal definition of love. Had it been wrong? Had it been the cause of my misery all of these years? Was it possible that I had somehow adopted a skewed version somewhere along the way?

Sure, Rochelle and Sandy suffered from the odd PDA at the most awkward of times (like while I sat here at the edge of Eden with this wonderful yet neglected woman, the last thing I needed to see was their tongues touching or Sandy sliding his fingers along Rochelle's bare-back toward the crack of her ass) but I could tell that their hearts beat for one another. Nobody else.

If that was what love was supposed to look like, no wonder Jennifer and I had screwed it up so badly.

CHAPTER TWENTY

By the time we left the party, it was a little after one in the morning. Emma hadn't stopped smiling all night and although I blamed a lot of that happiness on the martinis that Sandy had kept serving her, something told me that Emma hadn't had this much fun in a long time – neither had I.

During the drive home, I stole glances as frequently as I could. The wind brushed across her face and through her hair. It still amazed me that her husband didn't notice her, but something I was slowly realizing was that I only knew Emma's side of the story. I didn't even know her husband's name. I made a mental note to text her that question tomorrow once she was home – I didn't want to risk losing that happiness, especially since tonight was our last chance at fucking before she got on a plane tomorrow.

After locking up the Porsche and kissing it for the last night I would have it, I let Emma inside the house and offered her another drink, hoping she would take it so that she would be a little more receptive to my offer of sex in a few minutes. Unfortunately, she declined and said she would rather just get showered and into bed.

"I have a big date with airports and airplanes tomorrow," she elaborated.

I walked with her upstairs and retreated to the office while she did whatever it was that she did before getting into the shower. All that time, I tapped away at my propped-open laptop, adding words to a story that was slowly starting to lose its original purpose. How could I even think about reconciling with Jennifer after getting a preview of what real love was all about at Rochelle and Sandy's, after seeing how dedicated to me and my writing Emma was? I didn't seriously believe that Jennifer was the kind of woman I needed to spend the rest of my life with, did I?

And I was also a little distracted by the thought of Emma's naked body in my shower. In fact, maybe "distracted" was something of an understatement. Once I heard the water running, I couldn't even remember how I had begun the sentence I was writing. I honestly had to step away from my desk and start pacing, hoping to dispel those images of water rushing along her naked body, of soap suds swirling around her thighs and rolling over her knees and pooling at those pretty toes, the same path my tongue-

"Ah, fuck," I groaned and before I realized what I was doing, I found myself standing outside the bathroom door, my ear pressed to the wood. Listening in on whatever it was that women do in the shower – it didn't matter, she wasn't doing it with me and that was all I cared about at that specific moment.

And then the water stopped.

I hurried away from the door, letting myself back into my office and staring at the blank monitor. And it really was blank – the power-saver had kicked in during my soap-sud moment.

"Hey," she said, her voice surprising me.

I swung around, pointing back at the computer. "I was just writing."

"Get much done?"

"Yeah, a couple of pages."

She chuckled. Even I couldn't believe my own bullshit sometimes. I snapped back to reality.

"I was thinking of hopping in the shower," I admitted.

She shook her head. "You're not sleeping in the same bed as me. You realize that, don't you?"

"It's my bed, though."

"And I'm your guest."

"Okay." I stood up anyway and stepped toward her. She didn't move and I figured it was because she wanted me to kiss her. Once I was close enough, I stared straight into her eyes; she was a little shorter than I was, so she had to angle her neck to look up at me.

"We can't do this," she whispered.

"I love you."

She shook her head slowly, her eyes glued to mine the whole time. "You need to get laid."

I gulped and nodded. "Yes. Yes, I do."

This time, Emma punched me in the ribs and laughed, breaking the spell she had cast on me. "Getting laid is not the same as love, dork!"

We laughed together, but then our eyes got stuck again and I reached out and took her face in my hands. She felt perfectly sculpted to my touch, the way her jaw fit like a seasoned leather glove in my hand. And when I kissed her, my tongue traced along her lips and dipped into her open mouth. I tasted perfection, like a Lindt chocolate with that soft and tasty core. I wasn't sure what flavor would be "perfection," but it didn't matter because she wasn't a fucking a chocolate ball. In that moment, she wasn't even Emma, she was *mine*.

I pulled away first because I had been holding my breath; I hadn't brushed my teeth before kissing her and being a slight germaphobe I didn't want to gross her out. Judging by the dreamy haze of her eyes, I hadn't.

"No," she whispered, but kept her face angled towards mine, her lips slightly parted like she wanted another dose of my killer kissing. "We're not doing this."

"Sure we are," I said. I reached toward her again, but she stepped back and I was too lost in the moment to notice until I almost tripped over my own feet.

Before I could do anything, Emma shook her head at me, apparently pissed off all of a sudden, and hurried down the hall to my bedroom. I chased after her, reached for her arm to stop her, but she slammed the door before I could get to too close.

"Really?" I asked. I huffed at my bedroom door, didn't even try turning the doorknob (there was no lock on it, I could have stepped inside without issue). "Emma, don't let our weekend together end like this. Please."

"I can't do this," she said with the trace of regret in her voice.

"What's wrong?"

"Go to sleep, Morgan. I'm done talking tonight."

Dammit.

I looked down toward my toes (I discovered a new hole in my socks, just fucking great) and judging by my rock-hard erection trying to pierce through my pants, I wouldn't be sleeping anytime soon. And my lube was in the night table, right next to the bed in which Emma was currently laying. Fuck.

"He hasn't even texted me," Emma said. Two seconds ago, she was done talking. Now it seemed she wanted me to play the role of Dr. Phil.

"Who's that, your husband or therapist?"

I heard some laughter, but it was short-lived. "Why doesn't he love me like you do, Morgan?"

"Maybe he's fucking someone else." Bad, bad thing to say. I hit myself in the forehead after that dumb-ass remark. At times like these, I realized how badly I needed to upgrade my internal filter. Preferably to one that worked.

I heard nothing on the other side of the door.

"I mean, maybe the way he loves you isn't the way you want him to. Like you're expecting him to do *A* and he's actually doing *B*." Okay, that seemed a little better, but still no response from Emma. "Honestly? It baffles me how he never seems to notice you. You're funny, smart, tuned-in and just all around… I don't know… perfect?"

Some sniffles and then a faint: "Thank you."

"I mean it."

"You're a writer, though. Your words are malleable, replaceable, and by definition untrustworthy. They mean nothing to you and that's what I'm afraid I am to you, to Walter, to any man I have ever been with. A worthless word."

Maybe I was tired, or just a little stupid after spending the last few days in a Porsche that risked my ability to make my mortgage payments (or feed myself properly). "My words are malleable, replaceable and untrustworthy?"

"Think about it. Writers are always scrapping one word for a better one. Regular people just say stuff, they don't replace their words ever. It's the only way they know how to communicate. For you, you have a toolbox filled with words. If one doesn't work, you find another one. Or another one. Or another. You change your words like most people change mobile phones. There's no permanence, no commitment, nothing sexy about any word that you use. And that's what I am; I'm your words, Morgan."

She was wrong, but nothing I could say would convince her. "I had a nice chat with Sandy tonight," I said instead. "You know, he said if I ever wanted to get back into the bullshit of a nine-to-fiver, he could help me."

"Next you'll say you're going to sell your house."

It was a good suggestion, but I wasn't quite ready to throw in the towel entirely. Not yet. "I guess the reason I'm telling you this is because I'm an accountant just like Sandy is."

"Then why are you so shitty at sticking to your household budget?"

"We are so *not* talking about this right now."

"Why not?" she asked, and for some reason I envisioned her sitting up on the bed, crossing her legs and wiping the last evidence of tears from her face. Maybe the change in topic was a good thing – again, Mr. Brilliant Author to the rescue.

"Okay, we'll talk about this. The Porsche was to see how you'd respond to it. If it got Pretty Boy Jim laid, I was hoping it might work for me too."

"Oh, Morgan, I'm sorry. It's just a car to me."

"Now I know; a car won't get me laid. An expensive lesson, but I learned something, so it was worth it."

"You could have picked me up on a moped."

"And you would have fucked me?"

She laughed. "No."

I grinned. Obviously persistence would never work with Emma. "Anyway, my point about the accounting thing is that words are more important to me than they are to you and almost anyone else that has ever written anything. They're important to me because I'm good with numbers. Not so much with words."

She was quiet on the other side of the door. Maybe it was getting late; two-thirty in the morning and my hard-on had finally softened enough that I could get my pants off without risking a zipper cut.

"You're not my words, Emma," I said, standing up and staring at the door while pretending to be gazing deep into her pretty hazel eyes. "But you're my numbers. You're all of my numbers." I paused, listened, and figured she had fallen asleep. "You're my infinity. Good night."

I started walking down the hall toward my office when I heard her faint reply: "Night."

CHAPTER TWENTY-ONE

Airports suck. Emma kept her face turned away from me for the entire drive there. When I asked what was bothering her, she said she was fine. I kept my hands on the steering wheel, stroking the leather and looking for a distraction from her. It didn't seem to work because I felt a little insulted here. Not only did Emma refuse to acknowledge me after our fireworks-worthy kiss last night, but it seemed she thought I was stupid enough to believe that she was fine.

With so little time left, I knew that whatever I said to her needed to be fucking brilliant. I steered into the airport parkade and found a cozy spot. After killing the engine, I latched on to Emma's slim wrist with one hand and used my other one to gently rotate her face so that she faced me. A million thoughts rushed at me as I stared at those lips and hungered to feel them again, as my attention traced up her face to her eyes. I had to remind myself to breathe, just breathe.

Her eyes told me everything I wanted to know: she didn't want to leave.

"I don't want to go home," she said, confirming my thoughts. "Walter's parents are coming from Bermuda mid-week and I know that he probably did nothing to clean up and get our place ready for them." Huh, that last part sorta fucked up my theory about why she didn't want to leave; it had nothing to do with me. But I didn't let my disappointment show.

"Maybe if we kiss again…?"

She punched me before stepping out of the Porsche. "It's a good thing I don't have a bunch of suitcases. This car isn't much for cargo space."

I walked with her through the airport, remembering the last time I arrived here. Princess Bitch had promised to meet me and drive me home. Instead, she had ditched me without so much as a courteous call or text to tell me to find my own way home. That feeling of stepping into the arrivals area without someone waiting for me still stung because right now I could sure use that $50 I had wasted on the cab.

"Is Walter going to pick you up at the airport?" I asked.

She shrugged. "We never discussed that. And like I said, he didn't text me all weekend."

I shook my head involuntarily. It sucked living with Princess Bitch, but she was my first ex-spouse, my first failed marriage. Walter was Emma's second; no wonder she didn't trust me or my words. Assholes like Walter fucked things up for all of us. I felt like calling him and thanking him for my inability to get laid this weekend. But then again, it was his wife that I wanted to fuck, so maybe it was best that I keep that call to myself.

"I guess this is where we say goodbye," Emma said as we reached the check-in counter for her airline.

"No." I pointed at the TSA checkpoint. "It's over there. I'll wait here while you check in."

A half-smile threatened the right side of her face. I watched her from behind as she walked to the counter and I wondered what all of this meant. This weekend. Our kiss. Our plans for the Washington Romance Authors Event. There was a purpose to all of that stuff, I could feel it. And it wasn't just the sex that hadn't happened. It was bigger than that.

When she returned, she told me that there was no extra charge to check her single piece of luggage. So she checked it. And I knew, despite being the idiot that she thought I was, that Walter had no intention of meeting her at the airport today.

"You know," I said, my heart beating so fast I was worried that I might pass out. Again, I wished for an upgraded filter. "You don't have to go home. You can stay with me."

She smiled the *I pity you* smile that so many women seemed to be offering me lately. "My kids."

"Can't they share a toddler bed?"

Emma laughed. "I can't take them away from New York. Their fathers live there."

I pointed at the security checkpoint. "There are airplanes."

"You'd put a four-year old on an airplane every other weekend?" she asked, glancing at me sideways.

"It's not like they'd put her in the cargo area with the pets."

Emma laughed and hugged me. My dick responded, and I breathed her in like I always did and once again envisioned those lemon-cream cookies with the tasty center. When she pulled away, I held her waist close, pressing myself against her. I didn't rub, though; I just pressed myself to her and she didn't seem to notice or maybe she just stopped caring.

"My casa is your casa," I said. "You're welcome anytime."

"Thanks, Morgan." She kissed me on the cheek and started walking toward the checkpoint, leaving me once again with a hard-on in the middle an airport.

CHAPTER TWENTY-TWO

The rest of the month passed very slowly once Emma returned to NYC. We continued to text every day and chat whenever Walter wasn't around, but life felt gray, like it was always raining and cold and boring. Although it wasn't "literally" raining and cold, life "literally" was boring without her. I kept daydreaming about our moment by the pool, or the kiss, or our chat through my bedroom door, or the shopping, or driving the Porsche with the wind in her face. I sure missed the Porsche.

At today's marriage counseling session, I arrived on time (as per usual), which meant ten minutes ahead of Princess Bitch. With our extra time together, I finally admitted to Dr. Simms that I thought I might be falling in love with someone. He seemed to like this prospect; either that or the smile on his face meant he was ridiculing me, which was also possible.

"You know something?" he said, winking at me. "I was definitely able to detect a change in your writing since we began this exercise. It's amazing how love will transform the way you are, the way you tell a story, and your overall voice. Simply amazing, isn't it?"

I nodded, acting polite and diplomatic, which was a bit of a challenge given the fact that this part of my story had been written long before I arrived at the "love" conclusion.

"So tell me about this potential romantic interest of yours," he asked, crossing his legs and netting his fingers over his knee.

This was where things got a little awkward, but I rolled with it. "Well, she's currently in a relationship. I know she doesn't love him like she should. I'm very certain she loves me, actually. I think about her all of the time."

Dr. Simms was nodding and smiling at the same time, a perfect display of his coordination skills. "What does she look like, Morgan? Tell me what it is about her that makes you *feel*."

Okay, the though questions. I closed my eyes and envisioned her. "Dark hair, big boobs. She's roughly five and a half feet tall and when she smiles, the sun always comes out, even if it's overcast or in the middle of the night." I grinned at this part because it had just come to me. "When she touches me, it feels like home."

There was a tiny squealing sound that slipped from his mouth, or maybe I had simply imagined it. Either way, Dr. Simms' face opened up – wide eyes, a big smile. I could tell he liked the idea of me falling in love with someone other than Jennifer; even this objective, impartial marriage counselor could obviously see just how much Princess Bitch had stripped of my soul.

And then, as if on cue, Jennifer walked in, her iPhone already tucked away and a stern gleam to her eyes. Her presence stunned both Dr. Simms and me; his face hardened and he straightened his back, and I sat deeper in the loveseat, watching my wife settle into her usual spot across from me.

"So?" she asked. "Did I miss anything?"

Dr. Simms frowned at her as curiosity rippled his forehead. "Did you find time to create the next, uh, 'installment' in your Comic Book series?"

She didn't seem to like the question, even though it had been more than a month since she presented her last issue in the series – *C is for Cocksucker*. And while Dr. Simms had been the one who asked the question, Princess Bitch tightened her lips into a narrow slit and flashed an evil stare at me. "Is that what you want, Morgan? Your next single-page comic book story?"

I shrugged. "I can read again. I have lots more where my story came from. No worries." I reached into my pocket for the next folded chapter.

Dr. Simms added: "I think we're all enjoying your brilliant story, Morgan. You're a talented author, no question. However, this was meant to be a reciprocal exercise. Jennifer, you need to contribute if you want to save your marriage, if you want to see anything productive come from this exercise."

"Sure," she sighed. "Next week I will. I promise. For now, let's hear what happens between Oliver and Olivia."

Dr. Simms left it at that, then turned and faced me with an encouraging nod to get started.

And with their glowing anticipation pointed in my direction, I stood up, cleared my throat and continued reading from where I left off last week.

When Oliver entered the hospital room, he held his breath as his lifetime with Olivia flashed across his tear-blurred vision. The woman he had travelled across continents to hunt, to kiss, to make love to, to convince she belonged with him... that woman, stronger than the world's fiercest titanium, lay on her back, thinner than ever and on the verge of her very first and last failure. She had promised to beat this, had looked into his eyes less than three months ago and made him believe that she would defy all probability and become an outlier in this.

Yet there she lay on this bed, the last bed her fifty-year old body would ever know.

"Babe," he heard from the door. To him, her voice came across loud and clear, and strong and potent, in spite of the beeping and ticking and pumping of the machines tied into her frail body. "Come here."

He edged toward her bed, afraid that these twelve or so steps represented the end of their time together. He wanted to avoid those steps, as if once he took them he would never get them back.

"I love you, Oliver," she said.

"I love you," he answered, realizing that even though he heard her voice, her lips weren't moving. But her eyes were open and alert and watching him as he approached.

"I fought for you," she said.

He nodded. "You fought harder than anyone else has ever fought for me."

"I'm still fighting for you. I won't stop."

He choked back his tears, taking the final two steps to her bed. Standing close enough, he reached over the security bar and squeezed her palm, mindful of the intravenous tube. There was no strength in her hand, but to Oliver she felt like she always had. She felt like home.

"I know," he responded once he had his emotions in check. "You're my fighter, you've always been." He leaned forward and kissed her tired mouth, holding his lips against hers while he considered the next words he knew he had to say. At last, he pulled back.

"I will never let go," she breathed. Those last words were weak, so weak. Time was ticking and he saw the expectation in her eyes, which made it even more difficult to utter what he needed to say.

"It's okay," he said at last, his voice cracking as he squeezed her hand. He never wanted to let go either. "It's okay, I'm here."

"I won't leave you," she protested.

"Olivia," he whispered, his eyes wide because he wanted to see her, all of her, but the tears were coming too fast. "It's okay. Go home. I'll be with you again soon."

She didn't last much longer. A single tear slipped from her eyes as she blinked her final blink, a simple puff of air escaped as she breathed her last breath. And then she was gone. It wasn't so much that Oliver heard the single, steady beep from the machines, or even that her hand fell limply out of his grip. It was more that his heartbeat felt empty and the air in his lungs lost vibrancy.

For Oliver, the sunshine had gone away and it would never come back.

When I looked up from that page in *Our Story*, I discovered the tears pooling in Princess Bitch's eyes and the awe in Dr. Simms'. I flipped to the next page, ready to keep reading when Dr. Simms offered a pensive glare and cleared his throat.

"You're killing Olivia so soon into the story?" he asked. "That doesn't seem like the appropriate thing to do, Morgan. At least not from a literary perspective."

"He's an asshole," Jennifer declared, her voice as coarse as sandpaper. "A is for Asshole, remember?" She reached into her pocket and I thought she would pull out her iPhone, but instead she grabbed a tissue to blow her nose.

"Morgan," Dr. Simms said. "I think you should revisit your story. It's too soon. Maybe Olivia can beat this after all. Everything we've heard so far, the stars are always aligning for her. She shouldn't die, she's a fighter."

I shook my head, no. I had been reading during these sessions for the past five consecutive weeks. My novel had surpassed 90,000 words and this particular section was roughly the 75,000-words mark. So it wasn't "too early," not at all. And Olivia had to die. Without her dying, nobody would give a shit about the shooting star that present-day Oliver sees each year on the anniversary of their first kiss.

"I fucking hate you," Jennifer said from the couch.

Before I could dumb things down for her and explain that the finale was yet to come, she bolted from the office. She was done.

Dr. Simms and I stared at each other for a quiet moment, and then he asked me more about this girl I was falling in love with. "Does she live nearby?"

That made me a little suspicious. "No, actually. That's what makes all of this so difficult."

"Hmm." He seemed to think about it for a bit. The alarm

buzzed, signaling the end of our session. It was one of only a few times where the timer interrupted us.

"Do you think Jennifer and I will ever reconcile?" I asked him.

He sighed, standing up and walking me to the door. "Is that what you want? To fix a marriage that, to me, seems toxic and destructive and unhealthy for both of you, not to mention Evelyn?"

I remembered one of my earliest conversations with Dr. Simms' where he expressed a firm belief in this institution he called "marriage." He had underlined how long he and his wife had been together and called me out on the importance of a stable family unit, especially (or maybe he said "particularly") when it comes to children. His question today about whether I really wanted to save this shit-show of a relationship seemed to be a vague answer of some kind, but now it was my turn to call him out.

I asked my question using different words because I really needed some guidance here before I let my feelings for Emma complicate things even more than they already were. "So what do you think? Is it salvageable?"

Before he opened the door and kicked me out, he sighed. Yes, again. "I think anything is possible, Morgan. In fact, I also believe our government will pull our country out from its debt issues. But like I said a few weeks ago, if reconciliation is going to happen both you and Jennifer might be wise to do some self-examination at this point and determine the role each of you played when it comes to the problem."

With that, he patted me on the back and I was on my way out the door.

CHAPTER TWENTY-THREE

Since it was my weekend with Evelyn and I had a little extra money left over from this month's pathetic royalty check, I bought movie tickets for a matinee at the cheap theater and slept through the second act of some silly cartoon about birds that were somehow funny enough to kids, but entirely annoying to us adults.

Being an author meant a lot of late nights messing around on online networks and socializing with my audience, not to mention Skyping with Emma while her husband was out doing whatever and whomever. Occasionally, I might write a few paragraphs, but it seemed the networking demands of my new career had become more and more time consuming.

So it made sense why I needed a brief 1-hour powernap during the movie: I was exhausted.

When I woke up, I noticed that Evelyn had gotten up and wasn't beside me where she was supposed to be; where I had left her before shutting my eyes. In that instant, I sort of threw up in my mouth and the panic woke me up real fucking fast.

"Evelyn," I called through the theater.

Because it was a matinee and the movie was about to get released on DVD, there weren't too many people in the theater but luckily for me, there was a family of four (aka witnesses) in the row ahead of mine.

"Hey," I whispered to them. I had to repeat myself a couple of times before the mother finally acknowledged me, squinting like she needed to see my face in order to hear my question. "Did you see a little girl come by?"

The mother pointed toward the front of the theater where nobody was sitting. "Try down there."

"Thanks," I said. I felt like an asshole all of a sudden because it occurred to me that maybe the mother had been squinting due to blindness because, once again, there was nobody down there. Even a mildly blind mother could have seen that, so this one must have been really blind.

But then I saw something. A little head bobbed up from the seats, somewhere in the middle of the row, then disappeared again. The closer I got to that fourth or fifth row from the screen, the clearer it became. And inside my head, I groaned – *no*.

When I reached the row, I whispered (firmly, of course): "Evelyn! What are you doing!?"

The look of guilt on her face was priceless. Busted.

"Jeez, Evelyn, you're going to get sick."

Her cheeks were full, so I forced her to spit out the popcorn, uneaten candy and whatever other edible delights she had picked up off the floor and stuffed into her little mouth. What was she thinking?

"I wanted popcorn," she said as we climbed back to our seats. "I only ate the popcorn."

Right, because that made it all better.

Once the movie ended, I asked Evelyn out on a dinner date. She smiled but tried to bury it, staring forward instead of looking at me as we walked toward the bus terminal. I asked her if she wanted something tasty or something expensive, pretty sure she would opt for tasty since her mother didn't believe in fast food and I always seemed to be too broke to take her anywhere when she spent her weekends with me.

"Expensive," she declared.

I knelt down so I could be at her level. "Are you sure? I was thinking of sushi…"

She nodded, happy with my choice even though when Evelyn, Princess Bitch and I had been living together as a proper family unit, our daughter claimed to be *allergic* to sushi (like Twinkle, Twinkle) and as a result we always ended up getting something "tasty" for our picky daughter on sushi nights.

I shrugged. "Sushi it is!"

While we rode the bus home, I mentally calculated that it would be another two weeks before my next royalty check arrived from Amazon. And a week after that, I would be attending the Washington Romance Authors Event. There were two mortgage payments between now and then. I had just made my credit card payments. And…

Well, I *hated* being broke all of the time. I blamed it on the mortgage. After this week's counseling and some of the other things Emma had helped me realize, I wondered why I bothered with the house at all. Each time I made a mortgage payment, half of it went to the interest charges and the remaining equity would eventually get split between Princess Bitch and me. It made little sense to carry on like this unless Jennifer was going to move back home.

"Daddy?"

I admired my daughter, at the way her face inspired happiness in me no matter how shitty a turn life seemed to take.

"Are you sick?" she asked.

Her question surprised me.

"Mommy says you're getting skinny and if you keep getting skinny there will be nothing left. Except bones, I guess." She seemed to think about that. "Are mummies real? I don't know anyone at school who has a mummy for a dad. Are you going to be a mummy when you're just bones?"

She talked a lot when she was hungry and I felt a little guilty about not buying her any treats at the theater.

"I'm not sick," I answered. "I'm fine. I'm just worried about what will happen to our family, that's all."

"Like me, Mommy and James?"

Pretty Boy Jim's name grated on my nerves, but I kept my shit together for Evelyn's benefit. "What did you think of the movie?"

Sunday night when Princess Whore arrived with Pretty Boy Jim to pick up Evelyn, we were playing a video game on the Wii and having so much fun that we let her ring the doorbell a second time before I bowed out of our competition and forfeited victory. I had been kicking Evelyn's little ass pretty good that time and even though I *hated* letting her win like a spoiled dork, I suddenly hated Princess Whore a whole lot more for bringing Pretty Boy with her.

"Yay!" Evelyn cheered to the game console as she annihilated my character.

Actually, hearing that cheer and happiness in my daughter's voice was well worth the forfeiting.

When I opened the front door, Pretty Boy Jim had his arm around Princess Whore. Cocky fuck, standing there in his Tommy jeans with his arm around my wife's waist with that dickhead smile on his 5-o'clock shadowy face. I wanted to kick him. Hard.

"Where is she?" Princess Whore asked, stepping out from underneath Pretty Boy's arm and into my house.

As much as I hated doing it, I motioned for Pretty Boy to come into the very same house that he had wrecked.

And the cocksucker entered, too. I couldn't believe it.

"Nice place, Morgan," he said, glancing up at the ceiling and checking out the far corners like he had x-ray vision and could determine the quality of the house's structure. Who was this motherfucker, anyway?

"Thanks."

He didn't take his shoes off – neither had Jennifer, but she was always quick to point out that her ½-ownership stake in this place entitled her to do whatever she pleased. But Pretty Boy? He didn't own anything here, not even Jennifer. He was leasing her, it was temporary and he didn't even have a buyout option at the end; *Our Story* would make sure of that.

"You know, if you ever think of selling…" he started, but let the words hang there.

"It's not for sale. I'm managing just fine."

"I have some good buddies who are real estate brokers. They'd get you top dollar. And fast, too."

I ignored him. It seemed to work with the majority of dickheads – pretend you didn't hear them or read their texts, and they would go away.

Not so with Pretty Boy Jim, apparently. He stepped closer to me and my skin crawled – where in the *fuck* were my wife and daughter?? – but I didn't let it show.

"Jenny tells me you're not working," he said, keeping his voice low in a conspiratorial and fake "Bros before hoes," tone. Did he seriously just call her "Jenny?" She always insisted that I address her as Jennifer, nothing else.

"I'm a bestselling author, actually. I don't need to work."

He chuckled, stepping back because it was quite possible that my mental image of cutting his face had reached him somehow. Perhaps telepathically.

"I can manage," I reiterated once he was a semi-safe distance away.

Evelyn stomped up to us, her arms crossed, her lower-lip pouting. "I want to stay here, Daddy."

Another night couldn't hurt, but judging by the twisted rage on Jenny's face, she wouldn't agree to anything, not even something logical like two plus two equals four. So I appealed to Cocksucker Motherfucker Pretty Boy Jim.

"You want a night alone?" I asked him. "Just you and Princess?"

His face lit up at the prospects and I remembered those nights when Evelyn would spend the night with her grandparents. Those nights when I would get laid, hear those noises that Princess Whore made (did he really call her *Jenny?*) with each hungry thrust I pounded into her. Yes, my face would light up just like Pretty Boy's did right now.

"Not a fucking chance," Princess Whore roared. "Get in the car, Evelyn."

Evelyn started crying and walked past me, straight outside. She stood on the front porch for a beat, then spun back around and shouted into the house: "I like Corvettes better than Porsches!" She stomped away after that declaration.

Pretty Boy seemed slightly offended. "No way," he said, hanging his head and leaving the house.

Princess Bitch wasn't so eager to go, however. She glared at me.

"What have you done to my daughter?" she asked.

"A lot of people like Corvettes more than Porsches," I explained. "It's not up to us to brainwash her one way or the other."

"That's not what I meant. She never likes coming over. I have to practically beg her. She cries the entire ride over, she hates it that much."

"Really?" I thought about that. "We had fun this weekend. I… I don't know, I guess I showed up."

For once Princess Whore had nothing to say. She stepped around me and exited the house, but before she left, I chuckled. The sound stopped her and she glared back at me. "Did you give her McD's for dinner?"

I moved closer to her and it seemed to me that Princess Bitch secretly hoped I *had* fed crappy food to our daughter. Like maybe she wanted to see how Pretty Boy would react to the everlasting curse that human vomit left on a Porsche's interior.

"No, she had sushi," I answered. "And we also had a ton of fun this weekend. So the reason she likes Corvettes more than Porsches is that Rochelle's husband has a Vette. And if you think Jim is all that pretty, Jenny? Pfft. He's a rodent compared to Sandy. A fucking rodent."

She jerked her head like I had just smacked her. "If James is a rodent, what the fuck are you?"

I hadn't thought this argument all the way through, obviously. But I did devise a quick response. "I'm the one 'your' daughter wants to stay with for one more night. And that's all I need to feel good about myself." I turned and walked back into the house before she could assault me with another insulting comeback.

And for the first time in my entire life, it felt good to turn my back on Princess Bitch. In fact, I couldn't stop smiling for the entire night, not until I finally fell asleep at two in the morning.

CHAPTER TWENTY-FOUR

Once Princess Bitch and Dr. Simms knew that Olivia died at the end of *Our Story*, they didn't seem to care all that much about the last little bit of the novel, which Emma explained was the part that writers and editors called the "Resolution," or in fancy-speak, the "Denouement." Both seemed like fancy ways of saying "the ending." So on that last Tuesday before my trip to the Washington Romance Authors Event, I arrived at my session on time (yes, still earlier than Princess Bitch, as usual).

Dr. Simms took me aside and suggested we let Jennifer produce something.

"I'll be honest," he said, shaking his head and keeping his voice secretive, low. "I wonder whether she took this exercise seriously at all."

I agreed with him. All I wanted was to be a comic book hero, and Jennifer hadn't delivered. Just one more item to add to my list of disappointments. She always let me down, and not softly either. It was such a heartbreaking experience that when Dr. Simms told me that he would have a final recommendation by the end of today's session, I wasn't surprised or shocked like I probably should have been.

Before he could tell me what that recommendation would be, Jennifer galloped into the room, her face tight with anticipation. No iPhone, no purse (she rarely left it in the minivan because she feared it would get stolen) and no angry smirk.

"Let's hear it," she said before her ass hit the loveseat. "I've been waiting all week to hear how this story ends."

Dr. Simms clapped his hands and faced her. "Actually, it's your turn to produce this week, Jennifer." He seemed to think about it. "In fact, it has been your turn for the past eight weeks."

The way she crossed her legs and bit her lower lip, I knew Princess Bitch's veins had just cooled one, two, maybe even a dozen degrees. That blood had gone arctic cold in a flash, and if Dr. Simms didn't start watching his cake hole, Princess Bitch would rip him a new asshole.

"Yes," she hissed. "I realize that. But I would really like to hear how things work out for Oliver now that Olivia is gone."

"Yes, we would all love to hear the ending," Dr. Simms agreed. "However, it's your turn to contribute."

"However," Jennifer said, raising her voice a notch and not backing down, "I'm the one paying you, paying for this fancy room and cozy sofas and everything else you own in here, so I should have more of a fucking say in what we talk about. And I *say* we talk about the ending to Morgan's novel!"

"However," Dr. Simms retaliated, his volume rising to match hers, "this is *my* marriage counseling session and as the *only* qualified counselor in this room, I get to call the shots. *All* of them. And I'm calling for you to show up or go home!"

"However," she started, but I could tell that she had already processed his words and she knew, somewhere deep down (like so deep down that it was probably in the same dark and hidden place where she kept her feelings) that she really had no voice in this matter. "Huh."

Dr. Simms let out a sigh, a relieved one judging by the way his shoulders slackened and he sat back a little more casually into his loveseat.

Jennifer glared past Dr. Simms and made eye contact with me. She seemed to soften a little too, although my assessment could have been entirely imagined. "You're going to your writer's conference this weekend, aren't you?"

I nodded.

She stood up and said she had to get her bag from the car. Without waiting for Dr. Simms' blessing, she left the therapy room, bringing the tension with her. I wasn't sure she would return.

Apparently, Dr. Simms wasn't so sure either. "Tell me about this conference, Morgan," he said, breaking the ice. "Will you see your new love interest?"

"Oh, I don't think I will see her there," I said, chuckling and feeling my cheeks warm up with shame. I thought he had forgotten all about my little "love" confession.

"That's unfortunate. Does she know about your writing ambitions?"

I had to be careful with what I told him. I didn't want him prying too much because I was seriously in a state of mind right now where I was mourning the reality that she and I would never be together. It was impossible and it broke my heart, but at least I could still love her, I could still imagine what could have been. With Princess Bitch, it was impossible to love her and when I imaged what my life could have been with her, all I saw was heartbreak and abuse.

Luckily, before we could get too deep into a conversation about the woman I loved that could never love me in return, Princess Bitch returned.

"Sorry," she said. She stood on her side of the table, her purse open and a little out of breath. She reached in and retrieved a small stack of pages, which she proceeded to drop onto the table. They were the comic books from her series. She had not only created a new cover for each installment, but she had also used far more than the six photos Dr. Simms asked for when we began this exercise.

"There," she said, taking a proud little bow. "One for each week, so nine in total because I worked on an extra issue."

I could barely see the titles from this angle so I leaned forward to get a better view. They were obviously in reverse order with the latest installment on top and the one from nine weeks ago at the bottom. I grabbed the top issue and read the title out loud, even though the true appeal (to me) was the exceptional graphics. Wow. I felt like a hero again.

"'*P is for Parent*,'" I said, looking up. "That's sweet."

"Fuck off, Morgan." She nodded at the stack. "Let's get through this bullshit so I can hear your ending."

I placed *P is for Parent* on the floor and reached for the next issue. "'*O is for Oppressive*.' Hmm, that was last week's?"

She allowed an affirmative nod.

"Oppressive seems a little rigid, but the picture is absolutely amazing. You're an artist, you know that, right?"

She shrugged. The only time Princess Bitch ever displayed any hint of humility was when we talked about her artistic talent. Otherwise she was, well, a pure fucking bitch.

"'N is for Never Again.'" I chuckled at that one. "I completely agree with you. Nice one."

"Thanks."

"Moving on… 'M is for-'" I looked up and we both laughed out loud.

"Well?" Dr. Simms said, urging me to finish reading the title.

"I swear I didn't see this before I picked it up," I promised, then turned the comic book cover to him so he could see it. I finished reading the title without having to look at the words: "'M is for Moving On.'"

He smiled, but it seemed more like disappointment than pleasure.

I placed *M is for Moving On* on the floor and reached for the next cover. "'L is for Loser.'"

Princess Bitch shrugged. "They get nastier. I was a lot angrier back then."

I couldn't argue with that statement. She was always angry, but the intensity level at home had certainly tapered down twenty or degrees since she walked out on me. When I picked up the next cover, I caught myself holding my breath. She had used one of our wedding pictures on this particular cover. And while she had enhanced it with Photoshop or some other software by creating a false cut across my jugular, the graphics remained Hollywood-awesome, fucking breathtaking to say the least.

"'*I is for Idiot.*' Well, it sure beats '*C is for Cocksucker.*'" I grabbed the next one and read it. "'*F is for Fucktart.*' Isn't it fuck-tard? You know with a 'd' instead of a 't'?"

She didn't seem to care. "It's my series, Morgan. I didn't criticize your novel, did I? So step the fuck down and get through the stack."

I knew better than to challenge her; fucktarT it was. "'*E is for the End.*' Okay, let's see this last one…"

When I picked it up and saw the title for the 'D' volume, I felt a pain in my chest that made me question whether a root canal (without the epidural or whatever they're called) might be better marriage therapy than this crazy bullshit "exercise" of Dr. Simms'.

Damn.

Although this pain had been lingering below the surface for some time, seeing the title and reading Jennifer's words in a story that was meant for me… it all came with a certain punch. A hard punch, a

Tyson, a Mohammed Ali. And it struck me where it hurt the most, too: in the nuts.

When Princess Bitch spoke, her voice came out as soft as cotton balls. "That one is the bonus volume. I was probably at my angriest when I worked on that one," she confessed. "It was the weekend Evelyn said she didn't want to come home with me. The one where James came into the house and you and I left on bad terms."

I remembered it like it was yesterday.

The graphics on the cover had come from our wedding album as well, a photo of my left hand. Except Princess Bitch had changed the image so that my ring finger was missing, apparently ripped straight from its socket with loose veins and lumpy blood oozing from the open wound. Oh, and she also added lizard-like scales to the flesh on my hand. I chuckled. "I like the scales."

She rolled her eyes, the modesty from earlier still lingering.

Dr. Simms cleared his throat, breaking up the intimacy of this moment. "What's the title, Morgan?"

I pointed my attention back to the words and exhaled a long, defeated breath that could only mean one thing: acceptance. Yes, it burned me to see the title. After another deep breath, I read it out loud for everyone to hear. "*'D is for Divorce.'*"

Also this was the only comic book that I wanted to open up and read right away, partially because it contained several pages instead of the traditional single. I was fairly sure of what graphics waited for me inside that cover, but I opened the book just the same. What I discovered, however, wasn't graphics at all. Instead, I found words… hard, cold and emotionless words that painted a picture that seemed ugly today, but over the years would surely grow on me and possibly morph into the most beautiful imagery to ever stain paper. I wondered if some of Renoir's work had appeared ugly at first, too.

"What is it?" Dr. Simms asked. "It's so much thicker than the others. Tell me what you're looking at, Morgan."

Despite the sensation of having just had my scrotum ripped out through my nostrils, I knew this comic was the most transformational one in Princess Bitch's series. I looked up from the paper and stared straight into Dr. Simms' face while my peripheral vision detected tears in Jennifer's.

"They're my divorce papers, Doc."

⋆ ⋆ ⋆

After I left the marriage counselor's office, I found Princess Bitch idling in the van in the parking lot out front of the building. Once I got close enough, she opened the window and asked me if I wanted a ride home. Although spending time alone on the bus would have been helpful from a mental-health standpoint, I had a lot of work to get done before this weekend's big author event in Washington. So I agreed, and hopped into the van.

We didn't say anything for a block and even then the only reason she started talking was because I knew she had a tough time sitting still at red lights. She said: "I really wanted to hear the rest of your story."

"I'm going to be doing some pre-release promotion this weekend for that story. It needs to get to my editor before Monday, so I need to do tidy up the manuscript. You know, stuff like that."

The light turned green and Princess Bitch smiled. I didn't know if the lights were responsible for that or if she actually enjoyed hearing me speak about my writing. I wondered about that for a bit, but deep down it didn't matter to me either way.

"So you're sure about this?" I asked. "The divorce?"

She heaved a heavy sigh. "I'm sorry. I hate that this is hurting you so much."

I didn't quite understand how she hated hurting me so much yet she wanted a divorce. Okay, I realized that, on paper, between my formal education in Accounting & Finance and my current career as a bestselling and brilliant author I had no true qualifications in the realm of common sense, but if you didn't want to hurt someone, you had it in your control to not hurt them. So if she hated hurting me so much, why didn't she just move back into the house?

I kept my logic to myself, just in case she changed her mind about driving me home – I was close enough that paying the bus fare didn't seem economically worth it, and I didn't want to walk the rest of the way home because it was still far enough that I would lose too much editing time.

"You might not know this," she said, "but I've been seeing Dr. Simms on my own. Every Thursday."

Her admission surprised me. Maybe that explained why Dr. Simms had been so pro-separation recently – if he had gotten to know Princess Bitch well enough, he would have certainly caught a glimpse into the impossibility of her.

"He told me that you're seeing someone."

I felt my stomach tighten at the embarrassment.

"It's okay," she said. "I want you to be happy."

Another red light. Great. "It's really nothing."

"Does she have a name?"

I told her nothing.

"Will she be at this author's event with you, Morgan? I think it would be nice to meet her, especially if you'll eventually introduce her to our daughter."

I groaned out loud — this red light seemed to be taking a fucking eternity and the red hand for the pedestrian signal wasn't even flashing yet — like she were my mother telling me about the birds and the bees… at 25.

"I promise I'll be on my best behavior," she said, holding up her hand like we were Girl Scouts all of a sudden. "Before she meets Evelyn, I really should meet her."

I snapped a little and asked why I hadn't met Pretty Boy Jim before she moved in with him.

"Morgan, let's not argue."

The flashing hand on the pedestrian light promised an end to this life-long red.

"Is she pretty?"

"She's not real," I blurted at last, tapping a frustrated finger on my temple. "I made her up. Her name's Olivia and she's the lead character in *Our Story*, the one that died. Okay? Okay, are we fucking done yet?"

The light had turned green — I hadn't noticed the change — and the car behind us beeped its horn because Princess Bitch obviously hadn't noticed it either.

I felt the pressure building behind my eyes. When I mentioned falling in love with someone to Dr. Simms, I hadn't been thinking clearly. Because Olivia wasn't "someone." She was the *idea* of someone. The idea of someone perfect. She was everything Emma was (awesome tits, nice ass, flirty without being dirty, and all-around extremely fuckable) and everything she wasn't (so committed to one man that she ditched her place-holder once Oliver finally made his move). She was nothing at all like Jennifer – Olivia died, Jennifer was still breathing. In fact, the only thing these two women shared in common was they would use the same bathroom in the mall – the family bathroom which was typically kept a little cleaner than the public bathrooms. That was it.

"You're in love with an imaginary woman?" Princess Bitch asked.

Yes, I loved Olivia. Absolutely. "It was the idea of her. The concept."

She stopped the van outside my house. As I stepped out, she called my name. I was afraid to look at her face, afraid to find a smirk of ridicule on her lips.

"Remember in your story-"

"Oh, *Our Story*?" I corrected. There was no smirk of ridicule on her lips.

"Sure, whatev. In it, Oliver spent all of that time with his wife."

I nodded. "He was committed to the vows of his marriage," I pointed out. "He didn't want to be the bad guy, didn't want to be the one who left. If he left, his wife would have been the one who felt like a failure. Not Oliver, because he would have run to Olivia and his wife would have had nothing but her own self-hatred and disappointment. Oliver's a hero, he sacrificed as long as he could to spare his wife of those bad feelings."

Princess Bitch seemed confused. She wasn't an avid reader, plus she had no emotional intelligence whatsoever so it made sense to me why she didn't understand Oliver's reasons for staying, even though his wife wasn't always that nice to him in the story. Hmm, maybe it sounded a little familiar to her.

Princess Bitch nodded, though she was not entirely convinced. "But in the end, that's what he ended up doing anyway. He left his wife."

I shrugged. "He couldn't take it anymore and risk losing Olivia for good. Plus, waiting that long sort of backfired because his time with Olivia was over before it ever really started. That's the tragedy."

"No," she argued, shaking her head and letting the hardness flood onto her face. "The real tragedy was that Oliver was too much of a coward."

I chuckled. "A coward?"

"Yes, a fucking coward. All that time, he loved Olivia. All those years. Yet he was too afraid to break the heart of the woman he married, a woman he didn't even love anymore, so he broke the heart *and* spirit of the woman he *did* love. That's cowardice."

Son of a bitch, Princess Bitch was making a bit of sense for once.

"He ruined both women in the process – his wife for all of the reasons you mention, and Olivia, who ended up dying once Oliver stopped being such a big pussy and left his wife." She shook her head, a little disgusted. "If I were Olivia, I never would have taken Oliver back. *He* was the reason she died, not the cancer."

Speechless, I stared at Jennifer and wondered if our divorce was her way of leading a coward-free life. It hadn't been the first time that I wondered how long she and Pretty Boy Jim had been carrying on a relationship, but these days I really didn't care. Our marriage was over long ago, and today's *D is for Divorce* installment proved that.

"Maybe," she said, "you'll find your Olivia at that writers thing you're going to."

I wasn't sure whether I wanted to jump at her and strangle the life out of her or smile. Ultimately, I chose the smile because it didn't involve the police or a jail term.

"Thanks," I said, and then walked up to the house as an idea occurred to me. It wasn't so much an idea as a realization.

I didn't need this house.

It was time to sell.

CHAPTER TWENTY-FIVE

While I checked in at the Fairmont Hotel, I looked around and breathed in the excitement. Women of all shapes and sizes wandered through the vast, two-story lobby that looked like something out of *Gatsby*. They seemed to come and go in hordes and almost all of them wore event-branded swag — wristbands, colorful and cheap sunglasses, shirts, temporary tattoos. Some, I could tell, had been drinking and that was a good thing because I was told I always looked more appealing to women who were either drunk or passed out.

The front desk clerk handed me a small booklet that contained my room key and pointed me to the elevators. "You're on the fifth floor," he said. "As well, your accessories for this weekend's event have arrived. You should check in with the organizers before five."

I asked where the event was located and he offered a snobby scowl.

"The Spanish Ballroom." Like it was the moon and everyone knew where to find it. Once he detected my disorientation, he opened my room booklet and drew a line from the front desk to the ballroom.

I thanked him and took the elevators to the fifth floor. As I walked the hallway, I passed another group of women – a little younger than I was – wearing event swag and once they passed me, they chuckled. Perhaps they recognized me as the brilliant author of the *Sextual Encounters* series, or maybe they wanted to hit on me. Either way, I could smell the alcohol on them; it lingered like the overdose of Axe deodorant after you passed a group of fist-pumping guys at a nightclub.

After dumping my luggage in my single-bed room with fancy wallpaper and soft carpet, I made my way to the Spanish Ballroom. The room was spectacular – huge windows along the one wall with window coverings that were worth more than my life and chandeliers that looked like something straight out of *The Titanic*. Pure romance, pure elegance. Wow.

"Are you Morgan...?" one of the organizers started to ask, but I interrupted her.

"Yes I am. I'm here. Now what?"

She blushed a little. "You're the first and only male writer to attend this event. Welcome."

Her name was Natalia assuming she spelled her name correctly on her nametag, and she was a tall and slender woman in her late 30's with a tan that made me a little jealous. She spoke with a poetic tone and when she handed me my "swag bag," our hands touched and a brush of static electricity passed between us.

"Hey, that was like the electronic kiss in that movie, *Wall-E*," I said, which was a test to see if she had any kids. When she chuckled and agreed, I knew she did. "My daughter loves that movie," I added.

"Mine too, but it wasn't a kiss. It was just static electricity." Short of unbuttoning her shirt to reveal a little more cleavage to the one and only male to ever register for this event (me), I could tell she wanted me. "Will you be at the author's dinner tonight?" she asked.

"I'm looking forward to it," I said, winking.

She laughed that time, and then promised to see me later before nodding at the two female authors behind me who were waiting to check in.

☆ ☆ ☆

Alone in my room, I sifted through my swag bag to find a floor plan of the Spanish Ballroom. I located my table opposite the large windows, five spots down from Emma. There were thirty-two other authors who had signed up, so plenty of networking opportunities.

As I studied the names of the authors at the other tables, I wondered how the organizers managed to prepare my table without my input and creative direction. And then I tried to remember whether I had even seen my table all set-up and ready for tomorrow's "event" – a few of the other displays had been set up but I had been far too interested in Natalia to even glance toward my exhibit. Now I was worried, but not for long because the phone rang.

I picked it up to Emma's voice. "Where's your room?"

"Fifth floor." I gave her my room number and within minutes, I heard her timid knock. The moment I let her in, she embraced me – a tight squeezy hug that robbed my breath. It felt perfect having her back in my arms. What felt less comfortable was the semi-erection trying push through my briefs and rigid jeans.

"I missed you," she breathed, grinning and stepping back far enough so I couldn't arbitrarily rub up against her. I spotted the event tattoo on the inside of her wrist.

"Now what?" I asked, turning around and nonchalantly adjusting my pants so my stiffy wasn't so obvious.

"I thought we'd just hang out for an hour before I have to start getting ready for the authors' dinner."

"Is it a fancy thing?"

She shrugged. "I sent you pics of the dresses I was trying on for tonight. Don't tell me you don't remember them! Too much clothing?"

"The dark purple one?" I asked, and sat down on the edge of the bed because the mere thought of Emma in that dress made me light-headed. I also realized that I would probably be hugely underdressed. "Fuck, if you're going to look that good, I should go shopping."

She laughed. "It's different for guys."

"Why? Because you want me naked anyway?"

The smile melted off her face. "Pen pals, remember?"

I nodded, unbuttoning my shirt. "We're 'doing things right.'"

"Yes, something like that." She moved toward me and for a moment, I froze because I thought she would sit next to me on the bed and start laying down the foreplay. As much as I had fantasized about this moment, I wasn't anywhere near being ready. I would have opted for a nicer pair of briefs, I would have rolled some peach chap stick on my lips (her fav) and lit vanilla candles (also her fav) to set the right mood.

But at the last moment, she veered away and settled into the reading chair. I suddenly regretted my nervousness, but Emma seemed to like how uncomfortable she had just made me. Nice.

"Have you listed your house for sale?" she asked, completely changing the subject.

"When I get home, I'll be listing it." I patted the spot next to me on the bed. "It's more comfortable over here."

She shook her head. "You're incorrigible, Morgan."

I crawled off the bed and eased down onto my knees right in front of her. Not begging, but maybe a little desperate. I removed her shoes and started massaging her feet, which were freshly painted and way sexier than Jennifer's for some reason – feet were feet, but Emma's were... different than Jennifer's, and that was all they needed to be.

"Ooh," she said, her voice calmer now. "That feels good, that's really nice."

I moved my hand up her leg, and that put an end to it.

"Morgan! Stop it, dork!" She skipped out of the chair and headed toward the door.

I promised to behave, luring her back into the room. "I missed you, too. That's all."

She shook her head like I had a better shot at convincing her that the Easter bunny existed.

"Keep your hands to yourself," she warned. "Or I'll cut you."

I raised my hands like I was being held up, and then retreated to the edge of the bed. With her eyes on me the entire time, Emma slipped back into her shoes and returned to the reading chair. She didn't blink, not even once.

There was a silence between us while she continued to play this staring context of hers. It wasn't a bad thing – she hadn't stopped smiling for more than a few seconds since I opened the door and welcomed her to my room.

"We're not talking," I said. "Maybe we should kiss?"

A light chuckle broke her concentration and she looked away, but only briefly because she was pretending to not trust me. "Have you sent *Our Story* to your editor?"

I shook my head. "I will this weekend. I'll work through the edits tonight after dinner."

"No, you won't have time. We're going to a bar after."

I told her I couldn't. "I still have a mortgage and my *Sextual* sales are getting stale. Really fast."

"This is a networking opportunity," she said, almost begging. "You have to come out to meet the other authors, the ones with the bigger connections and readers and fans and all of that. If you can charm even one of them, your sales will skyrocket. Trust me. My book is getting published in two weeks and I already have fifteen thousand fans, of which five thousand of them are already committed to buying my book."

Wow. Her numbers were impressive; she wasn't even published yet. Those five thousand people could have signed up for just about anything, yet Emma had built such a strong author platform that she had almost pre-sold as many copies of her book as I sold, post-publication, in my entire first month.

"Put your work on hold for tonight and come out with the girls."

It was impossible to argue with her.

"Oh, and I set up your table for you," she added. "So the time I saved you on the table can be used tomorrow to prepare your book for the editor. Does that sound fair?"

I agreed with a nod.

"Good." Another staring contest. And then: "How are Rochelle and Sandy?"

We chatted about meaningless stuff like that for the next hour, never once talking about us. It was almost as if the woman from the text messages, pictures and telephone conversations was someone else entirely. Emma seemed different. I didn't understand that. And before I could even ask about it, our hour of "hanging out" came to an end and she said she needed to start getting ready.

"I'll walk you to your room," I offered, and she seemed to like that.

We walked down the hall to the elevators and I pressed the call button. Inside the compartment, I asked for her floor and pressed that button too. We were alone on the elevator and when I looked over at her, our eyes locked. It felt like this was the same as that first-kiss moment from back when she came to visit me. Fuck, I would love to taste her again, to be reminded of just how perfectly matched we were.

She shook her head, no.

I stepped toward her, yes.

"Morgan…" and just then, the elevator stopped and the doors opened for a group of event-goers.

There were four other women who crowded into the elevator and pressed L for the lobby. When I glanced over at Emma, she winked confidently at me, as if bragging about how successful she had been in avoiding my advances.

At the third floor, we pushed through the crowd and exited, but Emma didn't move much farther than the room with the vending machines and icemaker, which was located immediately next to the elevators.

"If you think I'm telling you which room I'm in," she said, "you're crazy."

I argued that it wasn't fair if she knew where to find me and I didn't know where to find her, but no matter how insistent I was, Emma remained firm and refused to tell me where I could find her.

"I'm married," she finally explained. "It's not a perfect marriage, and he might not love me, but I refuse to be that whore who cheats. And I won't drag you into my mess, no matter how much I love you and how much I really want to kiss you-"

"Or more?"

She nodded. "Or more. I'm not going to complicate things-complicate *us* for what will end up being nothing more than a moment."

She stepped closer to me and my body responded automatically.

"I meant everything I ever said or texted to you. Every word, Morgan."

I took a gulp of air. "Then kiss me," I begged.

And she did. She leaned up on her toes and planted a quick peck underneath my chin. "Now get back to your room so I can get ready."

Satisfied with the kiss – innocent as it was – I pressed the call button for the elevators and returned to my room.

Once my common sense returned, I realized that I didn't need to know Emma's room number; she would be coming for me before the end of the weekend anyway.

Dinner started with Natalia and her two co-organizers thanking everyone for participating in what was widely seen as the most prolific Indie Romance Authors Event in North America, but what else could Natalia say? As the only male at the table, I definitely felt like an outsider, but Emma was great at involving me in the conversations, most of which were technical in nature.

While we waited on our entrees, one of the other romance writers, someone that the others seemed to pay a lot of attention to and idolize, started talking about "Character Arc," and then as if she wanted to knock me off my bestseller pedestal she faced me and asked how it applied to the main characters in *Sextual Encounters*.

Although it was worth noting that I didn't really understand the intricacies of a character arc, I stared straight back at her and pointed out that all good stories were about character. But I didn't want to talk about my published work – I was here to promote my next novel, *Our Story*. So I gave her my usual elevator pitch – Oliver and Olivia meet by chance and have a heated non-sexual affair, but they both go their separate ways with the promise of someday getting together permanently. Although Olivia leaves her husband, Oliver refuses to leave his wife and over the years, he realizes how wrong he was to stay, and once he finally hooks up with Olivia, she gets terminally ill. And every year on their anniversary, he stares up at the sky and waits for a shooting star that tells him she is still there and still loves him.

"So, yeah, I think if you're going to tell a story about people, you need to place a lot of emphasis on that character arc," I said, watching all of the wide eyes on me – all of them impressed with the depth of my next story, all of them except for this best-selling lady who clearly did not like me.

"Your story sounds interesting," she said with a condescending snarl that allowed my personal nickname for her to burst into my head: twit. "So how does Oliver change? I mean, obviously he leaves his wife for this whore he was fucking, but is that really a true, deep-down change? It's just his character by the sounds of it and although stories are about characters, they're mostly about 'character.' There's a difference."

Well, it seemed I didn't like this author any more than she liked me. "I take it you've left a couple of spouses by now, have you?" I asked, chuckling at my own question. A few of the other authors around the table smirked and allowed some mild laughter, but one burning glare from this twit bestseller and they fell back into line. "The point is simply that Oliver didn't take leaving his wife lightly. That's where the concept of inner conflict entered the story. And it's through that conflict that he changed. Not just his marital status, but how we see him as a person."

The twit rolled her eyes. "Sounds like a lot of talk." She wanted me to jump into an argument with her, but what she didn't know was that I had spent twelve years with a woman whose middle name was Argument. Compared to Princess Bitch, this writer was a lightweight. "No offense, Morgan, but most readers can see what you're really up to."

"And what would that be? Telling them a better story than the same old formulaic bullshit they're used to reading?"

"That's what wannabes like you don't understand," she said, raising her nose a little as if to prove a point. I could tell I hit a nerve. Obviously her stories were extremely formulaic, possibly even reproductions of prior stories or mild plagiarisms of those written by other big-name writers. "Every story follows a formula. Each has a beginning, middle and an end. In some cases, the end is nowhere in sight and that pain lasts a lifetime."

I laughed. "Next you'll tell me that every Romance novel has a happy ending, too."

A few of the others chuckled or hid their amusement behind

their hands and napkins, but twit bestseller's face only reddened and tightened with frustration. Thankfully our meals arrived, providing a bit of an intermission to this silly duel of ours.

As I watched the wait staff place the plates before the others, I noticed that I was the only person who ordered the steak. The remaining plates were green or, for the daring among the group, white fish or chicken.

When the young lady next to the twit bestseller asked her a question that stroked her oversized ego, Emma leaned closer to me, placing her hand on my knee. The last time she touched my knee like this was to provide reassurance in New York after my lunch with E. Richard Kindall's intern. This time there was no reassurance; she squeezed my knee so hard that I knew she was annoyed this time. "You can't speak to her like that," she hissed. When I glanced into Emma's eyes, I saw a bit of pride there.

"Fuck her," I whispered back. "Who does she think she is? We're all indie authors, we all have a fair shot at having our stories told and sold and enjoyed." I shook my head. "I hate oppressors; I lived with one for a dozen years. And that bitch is an oppressor."

The pride in Emma's eyes quickly morphed into serious-as-fuck. "She'll ruin your writing career, Morgan. Step the fuck down."

I rolled my eyes and Emma squeezed my knee harder; it was enough to make me uncomfortable so I ate in silence.

Once the plates were taken away and dessert offered (and passed on by everyone but me), the twit decided to pick up where we left off. Apparently, she enjoyed looking like a complete idiot in front of her fearful entourage.

"You know, Morgan," she started, staring across the tip of her wine glass like it was the scope of an assault rifle. "I'm sure *Sextual Encounters* was an entertaining attempt. But more than that? I'm sure your next story about a cheater who leaves his wife will determine just how talented you really are as a writer."

Emma spoke up before I could respond and possibly stab that bitch in the eye with my dessert fork. "Morgan recently met with E. Richard Kindall," she said. It was like interjecting that the sky is blue in the middle of a conference call about economic elasticity. But Emma had a plan, I could see it. "Isn't that the same agency looking to work with you?"

The twit across from me seemed genuinely surprised as she studied me. I gave her a confirming nod.

"Impressive," she allowed at last.

"Yes," I said. "Either your writing sucks cock like you're suggesting mine does, or I'm such a talented and brilliant author that next year, I'll be sitting where you are."

No, she didn't like that.

✳ ✳ ✳

In fact, the twit (whose name will forever remain secret because 1) I still taste vomit every time I see, speak or hear it and 2) I know that oppressive bitch wants me to mention her name so you'll go and buy her shit) was so upset with me that she made sure I didn't get invited out to the club with the rest of them. And while my original intention was to sit around my hotel room prepping my novel for the editing process, I really wanted to spend a bit more time with Emma while I was here. Or Natalia if Emma was going to continue shutting me out.

Whatever.

Alone at the hotel, I went to work on my novel and got into bed a little before midnight after jerking off to Emma's older pics. She seemed to have stopped sending super-racy ones lately, replacing the nudies with selfies of her face (which was fine because that was exactly where I planned on looking while I fucked her anyway).

CHAPTER TWENTY-SIX

By seven the next morning, I was awake. After reading through last night's editing, I sent *Our Story* off to an editor that would make it shine, and then changed into my workout gear and hit the fitness center.

For a five-star hotel, I was a little disappointed. The equipment was fine, the change room was exceptionally clean and the sauna kicked ass, but something I learned about high-end fitness facilities was that beautiful, hot women used them. However, between me and the old man with boobs bigger than Jennifer's, there was nothing to look at.

This shit show did nothing for my motivation levels. The simple reality was that a first-class place like the Fairmont should know better. In fact, the lady at the check-in counter this morning (note to Fairmont: nobody checks in before noon because you don't fucking allow it) could have been more productive in the fitness room. It baffled me that the hotel manager would knowingly do this, so it was no surprise I ended my workout very prematurely.

By nine o'clock, I was dressed in a sports jacket and blue jeans, and I strutted straight into the Spanish Ballroom, finding my table immediately. I spotted Natalia off to the side, helping one of the other authors make her exhibit a little prettier with candies and keychains and swag that were nowhere as cool as mine. Both women looked exhausted and when I saw Emma as I passed her table en route to my own, I knew why. I had seen Emma like this once before – in New York, the morning after she passed out on my bed without having fucked me first. These women authors had partied last night. Hard.

When Emma waved, I tossed her a simple nod and wink. I mouthed a single word to her: "Tonight."

Her smile widened as if that was one promise she wanted me to deliver. And I would, too. The Washington Romance Authors Event would end tomorrow, and then it was a final farewell dinner, and early to bed for those with the flights at the brink of dawn on Monday.

At my table, I noticed several unfamiliar items – bookmarks for *Our Story* that I hadn't ordered, and two narrow, pop-up displays, one for *Sexual Encounters* and the other with me alone and my name in a font that was so bold, you walked away knowing two things about me: One, I was a motherfucking bestselling author, and two, I had a big dick (which could technically qualify as false advertising, because honestly I considered myself average).

I hadn't ordered any of the high-ticket items, but when I cast a glance five tables down, I saw a huge grin on Emma's face. I didn't know why she had done all of this for me, but it sure positioned me as a serious professional at this event. There was no question that I deserved to be here.

"Thank you, Emma!" I shouted, blowing her a kiss. "I love you!"

And with that, the ballroom fell into silence as all eyes pointed in my direction. Poor Natalia had to deal with it, so she made an announcement to say they were opening the doors to the public so get ready… it was time to brace ourselves because we are all here as leaders in the craft of romance writing.

That was exactly what I did.

✴ ✴ ✴

By noon, the flow of fans and indie aficionados slowed to a trickle, at least on my side of the room. I was surprised by how many people had visited my booth already. Most of them were middle-aged women and they carried fabric bags emblazoned with the Washington Romance Authors Event emblem. Almost everyone bought hard-copies of the books at the other tables but because I didn't have a "real" book for sale, I handed out *Our Story* bookmarks and collected email addresses. I promised each middle-aged woman (and the younger ones too, because I wasn't discriminating about who should buy my next novel) that I would personally email her once the book was available for sale. And as an added teaser, I offered postcards with random excerpts from *Our Story*.

One middle-aged woman in particular stepped up to my booth with her teenaged daughter (both of them such big fans the twit bestseller across from me that they wore shirts with the oppressor's face on the front) read the excerpt while standing right there at my table. Once the mother finished, she had tears in her eyes.

"What's wrong, Mom?" the daughter asked, grabbing the postcard and reading it. "Oh, heck," she said.

They hugged each other and cried for a bit.

"That's my story," the older woman said.

"Actually, it's mine," I winked, but I was dead serious – I hated plagiarists.

"No, really," the daughter said. "After she left my asshole, abusive, drunk-ass biological father, she found the man of her dreams. He helped her put the pieces back together again. He was everything to her, her air, her water, her life. But then he…"

Another group hug.

"Shit, I'm sorry," I said, and I meant it too. These two were close; I hated seeing the sadness between them. To make sure they bought my novel in the coming months, I decided to cheer them up.

"Listen," I said. "My ex-wife walked out on me after twelve years of marriage. No fucking reason. So I know how it sucks to lose someone you love more than life itself."

Sniffles.

"But you know what's really sad and, well, if you don't mind my saying it, disgusting?"

They leaned in closer.

"Those shirts you're wearing." I let that sink in, nodding affirmatively as they stared at me with blank faces. "I think we'll all feel a whole lot better if you head on down to Emma's table and get one of her shirts instead. She's way prettier, way nicer, and a much better writer than that bitch."

Their eyes widened as if I had just kicked a cute little puppy. After the initial shock passed, the teenager found my comment hilarious and she laughed so hard she said she was going to pee her pants.

In hindsight, maybe my comment was just a little insulting. Possibly even as offensive as kicking a cute little dog – the mother's dog, mind you - because once her teenaged daughter stopped laughing so hard, the older woman informed me that the twit bestseller whose face scarred her shirt was actually her sister.

Her twin sister.

Damn, I never was all that good with faces...

✶ ✶ ✶

Later in the afternoon, I noticed the author next to me. She was pretty in a petite, 5-years-younger-than-me kind of way. Not really my type, but I couldn't exactly let myself get too selective now that I hadn't been laid in a fucking-long time. Her name was Dawn Something, and she was cute (I probably alluded to that already) with her plaid shirt and capri pants with no belt that, when she crouched down, allowed me to see her purple lacey thong digging into her ass.

"You look bored," I said during a lull in pedestrian traffic.

She nodded and then glanced to the opposite side of the room, probably to where the twit bestseller interacted with a crowd of a dozen or so readers. "You were funny last night."

"Actually, I'm funny every night."

She chuckled.

"I'm Dawn."

I pointed at the banner laying across her table, the one with her name on it. "How'd you know I can't read?"

She chuckled again, and what I really liked about Dawn was that she seemed to enjoy my low-end B-game humor. I didn't have to try all that hard to make her smile, which suggested I wouldn't have to work all that hard to get her out of her pants either.

I leaned in closer, hiding a little behind my exhibit display so the twit didn't see us conspiring. "Did you go out with the group last night?"

She shrugged. "For a little. I was tired and it's not my thing. I came back early and did some writing. Nobody has spoken with me all morning. It's worse than high school sometimes."

I nodded at her stack of hard-cover novels. "Which one is your favorite?"

Dawn blushed, shrugging. She was indecisive as hell, but it appealed to me because Jennifer had always been a hot-head decision maker. "The one that means the most to me is *In Another Lifetime*. It's based on something that happened to me personally."

I didn't really care, but I told her I wanted to buy a copy. "As long as you promise to sign it."

"Of course I will!" she beamed. She grabbed a copy and opened the front cover while I found the right amount of money for the book. "What do you want me to write?"

"Let's start with my name," I said, placing the money on her table and coming out of the shadows.

She wrote my name. "And?"

"Your room number."

She hesitated, looking toward the twit's table to see how much of a mistake she was making, then said, "Ah, fuck it," before jotting the room number down and handing me the book.

I smiled at her, holding the book to my chest like it possessed my heart. I was starting to feel like this divorcé lifestyle was the best thing that I had ever been forced into. "Maybe we can write our own love story tonight, huh?"

With that, I returned to my booth and quietly applauded myself for making back-up plans with Dawn.

CHAPTER TWENTY-SEVEN

Although it was common knowledge that the group from the "in" crowd of authors was heading to a local hotspot where men dressed up like women and put on a show, I wasn't expecting an invitation to tag along or join them. So after the Author Event shut down for the night (at 7pm) I returned to my room and opened my laptop instead of heading out for dinner with the rest of them. Within minutes, my iPhone vibrated and I noticed a text from Emma.

Emma: Are you coming out tonight?

Me: No. The twit apparently doesn't like me.

Emma: Shit. That sucks. Are you okay if I go?

Me: Yes. Go have fun. I want to finally start writing *Sextual Encounters Deuce*.

Emma: OK. Text you when I get back?

Me: Yes please. I'll miss you like the stars miss the moon on cloudy nights.

Emma: Shut up, dork!

I started with a hard-core writing sprint and didn't stop for an hour, and the only reason I let up at all was because my hunger from not having eaten much all day was manifesting itself in the form of utter grumpiness in my writing. At least by recognizing that I needed something to eat, I couldn't butcher the story more than I already had.

Closing the laptop, I changed and left the hotel, surprised I didn't have to tip the employee who opened the door for me. I walked down the street and settled on a sushi bar that seemed new enough to know better than try to poison its patrons with expired fish.

As soon as I entered, a petite waitress escorted me to a booth and quickly brought green tea and a menu. It was nice to have this time alone and for a brief moment I forgot all about being a best-selling, brilliant romance author. But that moment was brief because I overheard some sobbing in the next booth. It was faint. Quiet, even. But being the sensitive, albeit fucking starving, author that I am, I noticed such things, which led me to peek around the corner of the booth.

"Shit," I said, staring at the pretty blonde. "It's you."

Dawn Something, my neighbor from the author event, looked over at me. Her red and puffy eyes made her seem a lot less attractive than she had been this afternoon, but those tears also hinted at vulnerability. "Morgan?"

She had already ordered her food, so I slipped out of my booth and joined her. "I guess you're not one of the cool kids either, huh?"

She didn't like my sense of humor; she cried harder. I obviously struck a nerve, so I placed my hand on hers to console her.

"It's okay." I breathed. "Why aren't you out with the others?"

"I don't know," she said, wiping her leaking eyes with the sleeve of her blouse. "After the event shut down at seven, a bunch of us were in the elevator and I asked what everyone else was doing for dinner. Nobody answered me."

"That's shitty. At least you got the hint."

She nodded, but it wasn't convincing me.

"You didn't get the hint, did you?"

Her chin quivered and she shook her head.

I chuckled, leaning closer. "Fuck. Them."

She half-grinned. "I suggested we could all go out together."

"What did they say to that?"

Although her half-grin began to mature into a full-grin, the tears thickened in her eyes. "They said they had other plans with [name removed to avoid a lawsuit]."

I stared off into space, shaking my head. "I hate that cun- uh continuum?"

Dawn chuckled and it relieved me to see a smile on her face. "She doesn't like you very much either, Morgan."

"That's okay. At least you smile when I talk to you and it's such a pretty sight that I couldn't care if my own mother hated me."

She softened a little at that. I was a romance author after all, I *should* know what words to use to get women to soften up.

The waitress came and asked if I wanted to order anything, and I did. In fact, I ordered two meals because I was starving and hoping that my display of eating a lot of raw fish would get the right message across to Dawn in terms of what my plans for *us* involved.

As if sensing my hunger, she looked away, and that was when

my phone vibrated. I checked the screen.

}i{

Me: How ironic...

Emma: Are you at the hotel?

Me: No. Having dinner.

Emma: Poor thing, are you all alone?

Me: A hot stud like me never eats alone.

Emma: Dawn?

She knew? I stood up and looked around the restaurant, but outside of a few Asian families and some college kids, the place was relatively empty. I didn't see Emma anywhere.

Me: Where are you?

Emma: Promise me you won't touch that whore.

Me: Aw, you're jealous.

Emma: She's a whore, Morgan. She's a whore who's engaged to be married. Probably looking for one last hooray before tying the knot.

Me: Perfect. I'm not looking to fall in love either.

Emma: But you have.

Me: I have?

Emma: Yes! With me! And don't forget it!

I chuckled and Dawn asked me what was so funny.

"Nothing," I said, then placed the phone face-down on the table. "I hear you're getting married soon?"

The way Dawn blushed, I could tell she didn't want to talk too much about her personal life. I didn't like to see her uncomfortable because maybe Emma was right, maybe all Dawn needed was to fuck one last guy before getting married and knowing, for sure, whether she really wanted to spend her life with one man.

"Technically, I'm married," I said.

She frowned and nodded at my ringless ring finger. "No ring?"

"We're getting divorced," I said, shrugging like it was no big deal. But it was a big deal. Whatever. "She walked out on me earlier this year. Took our daughter and disappeared until *Sexual Encounters* started getting some national attention. Then she suggested we try marriage counseling."

"I'm sorry," she said, and she seemed a little hurt that I had been dragged through this kind of drama. In fact, Dawn seemed to care a little *too* much; she rubbed my hands the way a father rubs his daughter's back after her first taste of heartbreak.

"It's okay." My phone vibrated again and I read Emma's quick text.

Emma: Right?

I pocketed the phone – it was rude of me to be texting Emma, who was happily married to some asshole that didn't know she existed and she was too fucking stubborn to bend a few "fidelity" rules – and focused on Dawn, my sure-bet for getting laid tonight.

"Yes," I said. "Divorce sucks. But the good thing to come out of it is our marriage counselor suggested that we write stories for each other. If we hadn't gone through that exercise, my next novel wouldn't have ever happened. Initially I thought I was writing *Our*

Story for Princess Bitch."

Dawn laughed at my nickname for Jennifer. "You don't seriously call her that!"

"To her face, it's a lot less painful to simply call her 'Princess.'"

Dawn seemed impressed. "After hearing your elevator pitch last night, I've read so much about *Our Story* online and then this afternoon when you were gone to the bathroom, I picked up all of your teaser samples."

"I was wondering where they disappeared to." I gave her a conspiring wink.

"So what happens after Oliver and Olivia finally get together?"

I told her: "She dies."

"Damn, I thought you were just kidding about that last night."

CHAPTER TWENTY-EIGHT

After dinner, we returned to the hotel. We ended up in Dawn's room because I didn't want her knowing where to find me in case we did fuck and she got a little crazy. Besides, if Emma came to my room and caught Dawn and me together, she might disown me. And as much as I hated Emma for not fucking me, I loved her far more for everything else. Yes, even though it took me more than 75% of the way through this story to admit it, I absolutely loved Emma, every last ounce of her.

With that little admission out of the way, I turned my attention back to Dawn who lay on her bed, propped up on her side by her elbow and smiling in her own sexy way. I wanted to join her, but sat safely in the desk chair, which was uncomfortable enough to keep me alert to Dawn's sluttiness. And that was a good thing in the (very unlikely) off-chance that I decided, at some point, that fucking her wasn't worth the trouble.

"So after Olivia dies," Dawn asked, "does Oliver go back to his wife and beg for her forgiveness?"

I shook my head. "No, he doesn't. He loves Olivia, even long after she's gone. He can't share his heart, he never could. It was always about Olivia, and that was kind of the point of the whole story."

"So the novel ends? That's it?"

I shook my head again, leaning forward because as much as I wanted to be alert to Dawn's sluttiness, my lower back was really starting to ache. "No, it's actually where the love story truly starts. Because we jump back in time and we see that the true love of their relationship started with one night. It was a conflicted night because they were both involved in relationships back then and in a six-hour period, they struggle with the things that two adults who want to fuck struggle with." I stared straight into Dawn's eyes and saw that she knew *exactly* what Oliver and Olivia struggled with. I gulped as she bit down on her lower lip, reached up and opened the top button of her blouse.

"So what happened? Did they make love?"

Fuck. My. Life.

I sat straighter in the chair, hoping for something, *anything* to snap me out of this spell of horniness. "Actually," I said, "they come to grips with just how much they love each other. They start making plans to be together. You know, like moving in and buying shit and stuff like that."

Dawn clearly preferred the part where they were alone for one night and had to wrestle with whether or not they should make love. Although she didn't button her top up again, she shifted in such a way that stole that extra cleavage from my sightline.

"The reality is that Oliver and Olivia hate the idea of marriage. They don't like it because they think it gives the other person a feeling of entitlement. Entitled to be dickheads, entitled to stop treating them properly, entitled to stop loving them the way they need to be loved. Having fucked up my own marriage, I can attest to the reality that once you tie that knot, all of that romance? The nice nights, the cuddling, the loving, everything? It goes away like Santa Claus on Boxing Day."

She frowned with a hint of fear in her eyes.

"Yeah, marriage blows cock, and that's what Oliver and Olivia agree upon when they're in that room together." I motioned between the two of us. "It's no different than this situation, I guess."

She liked that and let the shirt fall open again. My eyes traced her body, all the way from her pretty eyes down to her narrow feet. She licked her lips now. "So what happens between Oliver and Olivia, Morgan?"

"Well, after Olivia leaves her husband and Oliver decides he can't leave his wife, she tries to replace him. She tries to forget him, she fights really hard to push him out of her thoughts, but she can't. Every few months, they end up chatting and she realizes that love like theirs never goes away, no matter how much and how hard she tries to bury it. She has a relationship with some other guy, though, and just like she fought hard to forget Oliver, she fights hard to make her new romance fit into a box, but it never will. There's no such thing as perfect, she tells herself, all the while pretending that 'perfect' isn't Oliver, who's still living with his wife. This new guy treats her well enough, but when it's all said and done, he just isn't Oliver. So they split up."

Dawn let out a long breath, relieved.

"Oliver is happy about the break-up, too. But he knows if Olivia can so easily hook up with someone who isn't him, she might get into another relationship again. And maybe the next time, the guy will be good enough to replace him. And if he's not good enough, maybe she'll love him 'just enough' to never leave him. So Oliver panics a bit when she does find another guy, a really good one, and that's when he leaves his wife once and for all."

Dawn relaxed. "That's when Olivia *is* finally with the man she loves."

I nodded. "And they live a normal life, just the two of them with occasional visits from their respective kids. And it's about two weeks into their life together that they realize that true love *does* exist. They realize that the sun *can* rise each morning when they wake up and stare into each other's eyes, and the moon *can* shine each night when they share a pillow and fall asleep in each other's arms. They come to grips with the fact that cuddling *is* cool, that when you love someone, you don't care if her head cuts off the circulation to your arm and you can't use it the following day. Because that useless arm can only 'do' things... but the cuddling 'is,' it's love. They also discover that life was truly made for *two* people, the *right* people, and the world is actually a small planet when it's just the two of them. Each moment spent apart feels like wasted time, moments taken for granted. They live, breathe, and exist for one another, Dawn. It's love, pure fucking love, and nothing can take that away from them."

She let out a soft moan. "That's so sweet."

I crawled onto the bed with her, our eyes locked as I took her hand, the one her fiancé would have taken when he proposed to her. "And although they were always so dead-set against getting married again, Olivia will wake up one morning and look at Oliver, and in that single moment the world will just make sense.

"She'll say: 'Oliver, I want to marry you.' And he'll be a little confused and he'll laugh at her, and they'll make love and he'll think the craziness has been expelled through the passion and sweating and orgasming, and whatever. But when they're laying together in bed, their arms and legs entwined, she'll stare up into his eyes again and pick up right where she left off.

"She'll say in this long mother-fucking run-on sentence: 'I love you, Oliver, and you love me, and I know we both said we'd never do this again, but I can't breathe without you, and I just, well, and I just want to know you're mine, and I'm yours, and there's really nothing that stands in our way of being together forever, not paper, not divorce, not fucked up past relationships, not anything. I love you so much I don't care... I don't care if you're my second husband, hell I wouldn't even care if you're my fifteenth because all that matters is that we're together at last. I love you so much, Oliver Weaver. So much. And all I ever want, wanted or will want is to be yours until the end of time. I love you so much, all I want is us. This - us getting married – it *is* us. It's entirely us. I'm not saying you'll always love my quick wit, my silly meltdowns and occasional lunacy. And I won't always love you, because I know I didn't love you when you refused to leave your wife for all those years, and here we are, getting old together on a Saturday morning after making love. We *are* love, Oliver. We are. And I want this, I want to marry you because we *have* and we *are* what marriage is all about – we have and are Love. So what do you think? Can you marry me, Oliver? Can I be yours and you be mine? Forever?'"

Dawn was eating this shit up. And so was I because I was pretty fucking impressed that I remembered so much of that run-on sentence.

Her voice had dropped into the shades of huskiness, and when she asked: "Tell me what happens next," I wondered if she would be terribly offended if I kissed her, right here on the bed. I didn't, though. I kept my distance.

And I cleared my throat to refocus. "What happens next is Oliver shakes his head at her and says: 'Olivia, you don't want to marry me. You woke up today and realized all of what you just said and you thought marriage is the right answer to that.' He shakes his head and kisses her on the forehead, and it's fucking condescending, but Olivia doesn't fuss about it.

"Oliver continues, though. He says: 'I love you, Olivia, more than anything. I love you so much that I refuse to be your next ex-husband or another failed relationship. And the only way to avoid that is by never being your husband.' He kisses her again on the forehead and there are tears in her eyes, the same tears she wept when they made love that first time. 'Let's just sit tight and love each other before fucking it up with a piece of paper, hmm?'"

Dawn edges back from me, an angry edge to her stare. "What an *asshole*." Then she smacked me – not as hard as Emma could, but then again Emma never wanted to fuck me like Dawn did – and asked: "Is this when she dies and Oliver realizes he was a cocksucker? Fuck. Why wouldn't he just give her what she wanted?" She poked me in the chest. "Oliver's an asshole."

"But wait," I urged her with a slick smirk on my face. "It doesn't end there. And no, she doesn't find out she's terminal until later in the week. But that Thursday, the day before she goes to the doctor – and Oliver doesn't even know about that appointment – he's all ready for work and leaves their little condo while Olivia is back there getting ready, running behind like always. And he's standing at the elevators, waiting and thinking about how much he loves her. It's all he thinks about. When the elevator gets there, the doors open and he sees these people in their suits and work clothes and shit, and he realizes something. It's like that moment in a mystery novel where it all makes perfect sense. Oliver smiles at the crowd and goes back- no, he *runs* back to the condo like it's on fire, and when he finds Olivia in the bathroom putting her eye goop on, she turns to him and says: 'Oliver, what the hell? I'm going to be late.'

"But Oliver doesn't care about being late. All he cares about is this beauty staring at herself in the mirror, getting ready with a pair of funky scissors in her hand, and he sits down on the ledge of their whirlpool tub and just stares at her reflection, at her eyes.

"Oliver says to her: 'Olivia, from the moment I met you, you've filled my days, occupied my thoughts and captured every ounce of my attention. I feel, as I have always felt, that I was created for you. And you were for me. And I'm your second chance... okay, maybe your third or fourth or whatever. We've both sacrificed some of the things we love the most, just so we could be here for each other, in this moment – important things like sleeping in, like staying up until 3am on New Year's because that's when they celebrate on the West Coast where we met that first night after Chicago. We've sacrificed a lot, but I won't sacrifice you. You mentioned marriage this past weekend and I thought it just didn't make sense. Because that's what we always said – marriage doesn't make sense. But you know, those little talks were based on our past relationships. We uttered that disdain with our mouths, not with our hearts because our hearts were incomplete back then. And this... marrying you and giving myself entirely to you... and agreeing to take you and keep you and hold you every day of my life and having the balls to put all of this on paper and honor that piece of paper.... that's something that comes from the heart... or at least mine. Because I love you, Olivia. And I want to know what a real marriage is supposed to feel like, the kind where there's more love than anything else, the kind where a kiss at the start and end of any day makes life more than just worthwhile, it makes it pure and beautiful and absolutely the best feeling I could ever imagine. Olivia, and *not* your reflection – which is almost as beautiful as the real you – will *you* be my wife?'"

A tear slipped from Dawn's eyes before she threw herself at me, burying her face in my shoulder and just holding me. "I love it," she whispered, and then I reached down to her chin and angled her face to mine so our eyes locked.

We inched our mouths closer and closer until our lips were touching, and then we kissed like teenagers on prom night, wet and sloppy and full of passion until our jaws began to hurt and we were dry humping so hard I wondered if I had worn a hole in my crotch.

Dawn pulled her top over her head, exposing her 100% real breasts, her flat tummy, and as I reached for the waist of her pants, she asked the question that put an end to this madness.

"Do you have protection?"

"In my room," I answered. "But it's two floors that way," I added, pointing at the ceiling.

She reached down and stripped out of her pants. All she wore was her thong now, the purple lacey one from earlier and I wished, more than anything, that I could follow the exact path of that strap that started at the top off her ass and twirled its way around her core. OMG, I was so hard and ready to fuck....

"Go get it," she said. "Now."

I jumped off the bed, started to leave and then turned back. "Just one?"

"How many do you have?"

I smiled at her ambition and ran into the hall, hurrying back upstairs as fast as my legs would carry me.

✯ ✯ ✯

Once in my room, I hurried straight to the box of condoms and the first thing I did was check the expiry date. It seemed odd, even at that moment, to be worried about whether these things would work. But because I knew how my overly analytical nature often resulted in my giving up on a given task, I quickly dismissed the significance of that expiry date and rushed for the door.

But then stopped.

"No," I said. "Fuck, this can't be happening."

I closed my eyes and imagined Dawn. Two floors down, on the bed in her thong, ready to screw one last dude (me) before getting married (not me). She had kissed me so passionately that our chemistry literally boiled. I knew from my memory of her that having sex with her would be out-fucking-rageous.

I glanced at the packaging in my hands, an unopened box of [brand name removed because their endorsement check bounced] ultra-thin latex condoms. Having sex with Dawn could be out-fucking-rageous *twelve* times tonight.

As I began coming to terms with the benefits of getting back to her room, I stepped into the bathroom and noticed my reflection. My hair was a little messy from the kissing and dry humping, so I combed it again. I tested my breath, then brushed my teeth and rinsed with mouthwash just to be safe.

"Okay," I said to myself. "Let's do this."

I turned away from the bathroom, then remembered one last thing. Reaching down, I lifted my shirt and removed the felt from my belly button.

Perfect, I was ready to go.

And the last thing I remembered thinking before my evening took a viciously crazy left turn was: I. Am. Going. To. Get. Laid.

✶ ✶ ✶

When the elevator doors opened, my heart stopped. She stood alone, her face pale and her pretty eyes smudged a bit. She didn't see me right away, but when she did, she plastered a fake smile to her lips and I tossed the box of condoms down the hall so she couldn't see them.

Fuck.

"Hey," Emma said.

I was more than just a little confused, I was fucking speechless. Happy to see her, yes. Not so happy that I couldn't even fuck a ready and willing young woman without escaping the reality of Emma.

"Where are you going?" I asked.

Emma shrugged. "The lobby."

I stepped onto the elevator with her. "This is the fifth floor," I said. "You sure you're not full of shit right now?"

"Fine," she said, a bit of an edge to her tone. She refused to make eye contact and then she pressed the button for the third floor. Her floor. And Dawn's floor, too. "I was looking for the ice maker."

"There's one on the third floor," I pointed out.

Finally, she looked at me. "How do you know that, Morgan?"

"I noticed it last night after we took the elevator down."

We were quiet.

At the third floor, the doors opened and Emma started to step out, but I clasped on to her wrist to stop her.

"Hey," I said. "For real, what were you doing upstairs?"

She was half-in and half-out of the elevator, which meant the doors wouldn't close.

"Morgan, let me go," she begged. "I'm tired. I just want to get to bed."

I shook my head, no. "What's up, Emma? Tell me."

She rolled her eyes, yanked her arm, but I refused release her. She was strong enough to knock me off my balance, but I was still inside the elevator and we were still stopping the doors from shutting.

I used my flirty voice. "Emma…" And winked, for good measure.

She smiled, but didn't crack. "Don't you have someone like Dawn to fuck right now?"

Now it was my turn to yank her arm, and I was a little stronger than she was (yes I caught her off-guard) and she tripped into my arms. I hugged her, reached behind her back and pressed "5" for my floor. Once the elevator started its ascent, she softened, melting into me.

Holding her always felt perfect, but at that moment it felt like pure fucking heaven. She *fit* in my arms, she *fit* against my chest, she *fit* into my soul. When she breathed, I breathed (okay, neither of us had stopped breathing, but I swear if she had stopped, at that moment, I would have died right along with her).

"Emma," I said, using my chin to nudge her head and force her eyes toward mine. I didn't want to use my hands to nudge her because that would mean releasing her, and I refused to do that, refused to let go. "Look at me."

At last, she tilted her head and our eyes locked. The mood was better now than it had been when we kissed that very first time at my house. Way better.

Except the elevator stopped and the doors opened. We needed to step off onto the fifth floor.

"Let's talk," I said. "Just talk. Nothing more."

I took her hand, laced my fingers in hers, and led the way to my room. She didn't resist, object or put up any kind of fuss.

And just like that, the perfection of Emma made everything else in my world irrelevant. Which was pretty messed up because I had literally been minutes away from a massive fuckfest with Dawn. But here, walking through the hall to my room, then slipping into my room with Emma's hand in mine, I would have traded anything and everything in this world for a night of innocent cuddling. Just holding Emma in my arms, savoring the lemon-cream essence of her, listening to her voice, feeling her (fully clothed) body against mine… all of that meant more than a dozen lifetimes ever could.

Clarification: I meant more than a dozen of *my* lifetimes, because a dozen of Bruce Wayne's lifetimes was a completely different story.

CHAPTER TWENTY-NINE

We succeeded at the cuddling; Emma was the small spoon with her butt pressed up against my stiffy; I was the big spoon with my arms wrapped around her midsection; her hands held mine; my chin rested on her shoulder; her hair splayed in my face. The hours rolled by, lost in a gazillion conversations about life, love and lost time. These were the moments that felt as if they had stepped straight off the pages of *Our Story*.

Like now, a little after midnight, Emma asked what love meant to me. So I told her a story.

"I remember when my aunt Daniela left my uncle Liam. Now, Daniela was sweet and everything, always smiling at family get-togethers and always the first to come sit down with us kids at the kids' table. I'm sure it had more to do with the fact that she didn't like my side of the family and our table wasn't weighed down with bullshit politics and ass-kissing, so maybe it was just an escape for her. Still, Daniela made you feel like you were the only person in the world that mattered. She made us all feel that way. And then she left. My Uncle Liam was a fucking wreck, and everyone doted on him. I hated him for whatever he did to chase her away, but I also hated him for taking my family away from me. My parents were always spending their free time with him, helping him sober up, helping him move on, whatever it took."

Emma asked why Daniela left.

I shrugged. "I overheard Liam saying something about how she needed 'more.' Whatever that meant, because he gave her everything. Anyway, I never quite understood why Liam's world came to such a grinding halt. He couldn't do anything, couldn't go a few hours without breaking down and crying. Sometimes, we'd find him looking at CD covers and just crying his face off and when he noticed us, he'd ask what day it was. He was truly lost."

"Okay," Emma said. I could tell she was getting tired. "That sounds like love. Not being able to exist without the person you love.

When your spirit breaks and the physical world lacks any relevance. Have you ever known love like that, Morgan?"

"That's where it gets interesting," I said. "Because what I figured out from watching Uncle Liam was that he built his entire life around Daniela. Everything he ever did involved her. Those CD's he bought and listened to… with her. That house he lived in… with her. Going to work, he would talk on his cell phone… with her. Every spare moment was spent… with her. It was so bad that even when he hung out with us, his own fucking family, it was time spent… with her."

"She was his Everything," Emma said and I could feel her smiling. "That's perfect, don't you think?"

"No, it's an illusion. Uncle Liam was addicted. And like all addictions, the only way to survive is by detaching and distancing yourself from the people and things that remind you of that addiction. In his case, he needed to avoid being tempted to *think* about her."

"Addiction is a physiological condition, but love is a heart condition," she said. Heart condition? I didn't buy it.

"He sold the house, got a new job, a new car, moved to Canada of all fucking places and we didn't see him for years. We received letters, old-fashion letters that he sent in the mail, and sometimes I'd read them. He didn't even own a computer because whenever

Daniela was away, they would chat through Skype… on his computer. And owning a new computer would only tempt him to think about her again. That's how you deal with addiction – you remove those temptations, right?"

I felt Emma stiffen in my arms. "This is turning into a sad story, isn't it?"

"No, it's the opposite. It's a story of survival because all of that physical change and displacement was necessary for Uncle Liam to evolve beyond Daniela. And that's how he became normal again. Now he's loaded in his little igloo and Reebok snowshoes."

She laughed. "Really? He lives in an igloo?"

"I don't think so. I know he has a place in the Bahamas, though. He drives an Audi in Canada, has fractional jet ownership and sends me a grand every year for Christmas. Me and all of my cousins. My Dad says Uncle Liam can't spend it all, even after the Canadian government rapes him on taxes to support their socialist causes."

"They're not socialists, dork!" She jabbed me in the ribs.

"Uncle Liam says they are. Anyway, his survival has been an important lesson for me these past few months."

"Lesson… in what way?"

"You have a shitty memory, don't you?"

"Fuck you, Morgan." Another jab and it became playful for a minute or two until I planted my face against her warm neck, my lips itching to kiss her but my brain warning me that if I fucked this up, she would grab her things and leave. And since I highly doubted that Dawn was still awake and waiting for me to come and fuck her, I preferred this innocent cuddling to spending the night alone.

"You asked about love," I reminded her. "And that's what I've learned about it since Jennifer picked up and moved out, just like Daniela walked out on Uncle Liam. It's not real. Love is a product of habit and routine. If you break that habit and change those routines, the person you've loved and lost and can't live without suddenly becomes an easy memory to file in the back of your mind. In other words, love isn't a heart condition. It's not even an emotional one. It's just a four-letter word we use when we want to control someone else and ruin their life if we ever decide to walk out on them."

Emma didn't speak. We cuddled in silence for a few minutes when she asked: "What about Rochelle and Sandy? Unlike your uncle, these two are still together."

"But either one of them can walk out on the other. The remaining spouse will be crushed, but not dead. Just change your habits and start new routines and, hallelujah, you're saved, reborn, whatever."

More silence.

"I swear, I've always wanted to be loved," I said. "Like the love Uncle Liam had. Like the love I thought I had with Jennifer. Like the love between Olivia and Oliver in *Our Story*. But it just doesn't exist."

Emma sniffled, but when I lifted myself up and checked in on her, I noticed that her eyes were dry. "That's sad, Morgan. It's the saddest thing I've ever heard, actually."

Now it was my turn to go speechless.

"Is that what you really believe about love?"

I gave it some thought, and it didn't take much for the imagery of heartbreak to crash across the movie screen in my head. If love existed, I wondered how Jennifer could have hurt me like she did; how Walter could neglect this woman in my arms; how Dawn could have so easily slept with me, someone she had known less than 48 hours when she and her fiancé were approaching their wedding day.

When I failed to respond, she peeled herself out of my arms and rolled out of bed. "I need to go," she said. "I need to shower. And sleep."

I walked with her to the door, aware that I didn't want to sleep alone but not sure how I could turn this around. And then I blurted out: "Why don't you shower and sleep here?"

With her hand on the doorknob, she asked why.

I shrugged. "I don't want to be alone."

She didn't move and her immobility suggested she was thinking about it.

"Nothing will happen. I won't hurt you, I won't lose you. I promise." I waved over my shoulder at somewhere in my room, hoping she could see my open suitcase sharing the desk with my laptop computer. "I have boxers and a t-shirt you can wear. Just don't leave." I exhaled a long breath of air, exhausted. "I'm tired of people walking out on me."

That sealed it. She allowed a compassionate nod. "Get me the boxers and t-shirt. Make sure they're clean and I'll stay. Just tonight. I'll stay."

I couldn't help but smile as I backed into the room, fetching the clothes I had promised. "Thank you."

"Nothing will happen, Morgan."

"I promise," I said. "Nothing will happen."

I realized, somewhere around 4:00am that I was horrible at keeping promises, because nothing didn't happen. Double-negatives translation: something happened. Well, not just "something," but everything.

Once Emma finished in the shower, I texted her our secret code word.

}i{

And when she came to bed, she suggested I shower as well because she hated the idea that I had eaten dinner with Dawn (in reality, she didn't use Dawn's name but simply referred to her as a "dirty, raunchy whore," which were *her* words, as evidenced by the quotation marks).

Unlike Emma who refused to let me see her naked, I showered and air-dried on my walk back through the room to my suitcase.

"Morgan! You're naked!"

"You've seen it all before," I reminded her.

"Come on!" she squealed and then buried her head in her pillow. "Tell me once you're dressed! I'm tired."

I grabbed a fresh pair of briefs and a t-shirt.

Turned out the lights.

Slipped into the sheets.

Spooned into Emma again because it felt so fucking perfect. Plus I refused to let go. This would never become one of those memories that I would ever file away under "lost time." This was the *only* time.

Then her legs wrapped around mine, and at first, I felt every muscle in my body tense because I didn't want to fuck this up, didn't want to get the wrong message. I quickly relaxed as Emma's fingers slithered between mine, and she turned her head and pressed her lips against mine, and then she rolled onto me so her pubic bone pressed against mine, and then I caught myself massaging her big fake boobs, her nipples becoming firm instantly, our hips grinding, and then she was on her back, panting, saying my name, my hands gripping the waist of her boxers- no, *my* boxers (which she was wearing) and she lifted her hips to help, and I repossessed my boxers, exposing her, all of her.

"Morgan," she breathed, opening her legs for me.

I took her leg and kissed and licked and traced a perfect, soft path all the way up to her }i{ where I hesitated, knowing that if I started I will never...

"Stop," she said. "I'm married."

My eyes locked onto hers while I forgot all about my hands, abandoned on the inside of her knees, her skin warm against my palms. Once I remembered that she said *Stop*, I looked down, straight between her legs and realized how quickly I had almost ruined everything. What had I been thinking?

But as I started to draw my hands back, I felt her fingers slither into my hair.

She wasn't pulling me away, she was pushing me closer. I obeyed. My lips kissed the inside of her thighs, getting a taste of her smooth skin, but she guided me to her core. I kissed her there, too, but once her breath hitched, I wanted more. So I used my tongue and traced the length of her, shallow on the first pass, then deeper the next time, and deeper yet the third time, and before I could even keep count anymore, my thumb was massaging her button in a gentle circular motion while my tongue dove deeper and deeper inside her, reaching and hungry and insatiable.

She moaned once, twice, and then said my name.

"Stop," she breathed. "We can't."

This time, she *pulled*. She brought my lips to hers and kissed me like I had just died and she was that angel waiting for me at the gates of heaven.

"I love you," she whimpered, and her feet hitched around the waist of my briefs and pushed them down the length of my legs.

There was a moment while I lay on top of her, both of us naked and so lost in the moment that nothing made sense anymore. As I stared into her pleading eyes, I could tell she needed me to make the decision here. Either we stopped now and wondered "what if" for the rest of our lives, or we did what Oliver and Olivia did that special night, the night that changed their lives, ruined them and transformed them from a woman – a woman who fought for love – and a man – a man who spent the rest of his life chasing shooting stars once a year – into one single spiritual entity.

Right or wrong, I loved *Our Story*; things had worked out for Oliver and Olivia and I knew Emma loved the story too, so I gambled on the assumption that things would work out for us too. Right or wrong, I also loved my dick, which I grabbed with my free hand and, still staring into Emma's moist eyes, stroked my head along her wet, swollen }i{ .

"I love you, Emma," I whispered, and with that, she closed her eyes and rolled her hips, sliding herself easily and gently onto me.

Right or wrong, I loved Emma as best as I could for someone who just thirty minutes prior had claimed to not believe in love.

Right or wrong?

Seriously?

No.

It was wrong. Every thrust, every moan, every kiss, every quiver and toe curl. It was all so very wrong, no matter how right and perfect and ecstatic it seemed in the moment.

Wrong, wrong, wrong.

I just didn't know it yet.

CHAPTER THIRTY

That night, after Emma and I fucked, I had one hell of a messed-up dream. In it, I lived in something of a valley, in a big house on the river with lots of windows and a flat roof, an architectural beauty that would easily get me laid if I were living in the 80's. Because the house was located in a valley, my driveway was a bit of a hike up a hill. Nothing crazy; it wasn't like I needed a chair-lift like they had on the ski slopes that Uncle Liam evidently frequented.

In this dream, Emma had come to visit me and she was ready to go home, so we left the house together and I accompanied her for the hike up this little hill, all the way to where she had parked her car, which wasn't a Volkswagen, but a Land Rover. The choice of vehicle didn't make sense, but it was a dream. And just like I hadn't had much control over the sex that had happened prior to this dream, I didn't have much input into the type of car she drove.

We packed her things into the back of the Land Rover, and it seemed like a lot of stuff — an armoire, sofa, gun safe, two suitcases and one of those inflatable pools that put smiles on toddlers' faces. Again, it was a dream, albeit a messed-up one.

"I love you," I said to her, and she smiled up at me.

"I love you too."

I took her face with my hands and kissed her lips. It was an innocent kiss with no tongue, the kind of affection I might have shown Daniela at one of those family functions.

"That's it?" she asked, still smiling.

In my dream, I had a million thoughts running through my head — namely that I wanted her to come visit me again — but all I managed was: "I love you."

She chuckled. "I love you too."

We hugged, a deep and powerful hug that had goodbye written all over it and in the dream I suddenly felt sad. I knew this was the end. Fuck. The skies became grey, dark and I knew that if I didn't focus on her face, she would turn into a guy or Jennifer or Dawn or *anyone else* except Emma.

"I love you," I said, but I really meant to say, "See you again, right?"

"Yes," she answered, still smiling and it was starting to freak me out. "I'll be home tonight."

Home?

Then she turned and stepped into the Land Rover.

I walked away, back down into the valley and just before I opened the front door to my 1980's-chic house, I glanced back up the hill and spotted Emma there. Well, not Emma, but the Land Rover. I wondered what she was doing but there was a glimmer of pre-rainstorm sunlight that reflected off the Rover's windows so I couldn't see inside the cabin. I couldn't tell if she was watching me, texting someone, talking on the phone, crying… I just couldn't tell, and it bothered me. But instead of running after her, I stepped inside my house.

What were you doing, Emma?

And inside my house, Oliver from *Our Story* greeted me in a butler's outfit.

"I love you," I said, but meant, "What the fuck are you doing here?"

He gave me a nod. "Sir, you should have run after her. If it were Olivia, I would have chased after her for as long as I had to, until she stopped or ran out of gas." He looked up to the ceiling and pointed at what I assumed was an imaginary shooting star. "I'm still chasing after her."

Right away, I knew I had made a big mistake. And because the alarm went off in real-life, I didn't even have any dream-time left to fix the mistake I had made.

Yes, it was going to be the worst day of my life.

☆ ☆ ☆

When I opened my eyes, I noticed that Emma was still asleep in spite of my phone's alarm vibrating and chiming like a colicky infant. After disarming the iPhone, I lay in bed and watched her sleep, watched her breathe. I couldn't help but smile, even though in my dream she seemed to have slipped through my fingers and evaporated like water.

I reached out and brushed a few strands of loose hair from her face, and in her sleep she gave a twitchy smile. And then I watched a little more, even though the author's event was schedule to open to the public again in…

I grabbed the phone to see the time. Yes, the event would open in less than half an hour. But I also noticed that I had a text message from Emma. I unlocked the iPhone and activated the text messaging app. Her message came last night while I was in the shower. It read simply:

}i{

I grinned at this text because it belonged to us alone. It was one thing I didn't have to share with anyone else. But when it struck me that tomorrow she would get on a plane and fly back to Walter, I became sad. Placing my phone on the table next to the bed, I stared at Emma for a good ten minutes, memorizing every detail of her face, the creases around her mouth, the lines at the corners of her eyes, the curve of her nose, the bulge of her lips, and then when I figured I would never forget this simple moment in my life, I reached out and shook her gently awake.

She smiled when she saw me, then cuddled into me, kissing me on the chin.

"Does my breath stink?" she asked.

"I wouldn't care if it did," I answered, and then tried for her lips, but she pulled back and shook her head.

"How long before we need to be downstairs?" she asked.

I climbed on top of her, but she felt rigidly defensive beneath me.

"I should get ready." She squirmed, trying to fight her way out of the cage I created around her with my body. "I can't go like this, dressed in your clothes."

I let her out. "Emma," I whined.

"What?" she asked as she slipped into her clothes from last night.

Something had changed. I stepped out of bed and walked up to her, but I knew better than to reach down for those hands that fit so perfectly in mine. "Is everything okay? Did I do something?" Because I happened to be one of those guys that did lots of horrible things while he was asleep of course. What the fuck had changed?

When she finally met my glare, I discovered tears. They weren't the happy kind, either.

And I realized that our special symbol - }i{ - meant something entirely different for her than it meant for me.

✯ ✯ ✯

The only person with a bit of life in the Spanish Ballroom was Natalia. She seemed to have a permanent smile and endless Washington Romance Authors Event stamina. Even the bestselling twit in the booth across from mine looked exhausted and ready for a long, long nap.

When Dawn arrived, I chanced a glance at her, but she refused to look at me.

"Hey," I said.

She crossed her arms as she sat down and stared straight forward, clearly pissed that I never returned to her room last night after I ran off to fetch protection. I considered suggesting to her that the best protection was abstinence, but because she refused to acknowledge me, I let it go.

"Gonna be a long day if we're not talking, neighbor."

Still nothing.

I stood up and walked over to her booth, but I may as well have been invisible.

"Dawn, listen."

That did it. She turned her attention to me, allowing me a glimpse into the demonic anger that would no doubt haunt her future husband to his grave if he ever fucked up. "Morgan, you're an asshole. If you flew here, I hope your plane crashes."

I shook my head. "No, I didn't fly."

"Then I hope your car blows up."

"Actually, I didn't drive either."

"Stop," she said, letting the volume rise just enough for our immediate neighbors to detect the tension between us. "If you so much as look at me today, I swear I'll yell 'rape.'"

I stepped back.

"Leave. Me. Alone."

I wondered if any gray area existed in what she had just said, whether there was a loophole somewhere that might allow me to misinterpret her request.

I glanced farther down the line of authors and spotted Emma slouching in her chair. It felt like I had nobody on my side anymore, which was a lonely feeling after the rush of emotion I had experienced between Emma's legs last night.

"Okay," I said. I let out a tired sigh, straightened my back and kept my chin up. "Okay."

I returned to my table and put on a smile for the first few fans that wandered over to see me.

✯ ✯ ✯

Later in the afternoon, with a couple of hours left in the Authors Event, I noticed Emma stepping away from her booth during a lull in traffic. I glanced across the room and noticed the twit bestseller observing me, her eyes narrowed into angry slits. Those eyes jumped between Emma and me until something seemed to click in her head – I could almost smell the smoke from all the hard work going on in her little brain.

I remembered the advice Oliver had given me in my dream – he would have chased Olivia. Maybe this was my opportunity.

Fuck it.

I left the table and sprinted after Emma. Once I made it out of the Spanish Ballroom, I veered toward the bathrooms, making it with just enough time to watch Emma enter the women's room. Out of reach.

I couldn't believe my luck today.

Waiting outside the bathroom doors, I tried to make sense of what had happened between us. Okay, maybe she was a little disappointed in my performance. Admittedly, the sex hadn't been the best performance of my life. As a guy who liked to fuck, I was one of those performers that got better with time. Like wine or the price of gold. And since it was our first time together, I also acknowledged that our sexual encounter probably lacked steaminess; if EL James had put our sex scene in *Fifty Shades*, her editor would have suggested changing Christian Gray's name to Christian Lame. But two months from now as Emma and I worked on it, we could probably write our own soft porn books.

Or maybe it wasn't the performance. Maybe Emma simply wasn't attracted to me. But no, that didn't make any sense because we had chemistry and we *worked*. This attitude problem of hers was pretty fucking confusing.

When she emerged from the bathroom with tears in her eyes and saw me, anger quickly possessed her face. She tried to walk past me, as if I might truly be stupid enough to let her go.

I grabbed her wrist, just like I had that weekend she had come to visit me. "Emma, what's really going on?"

I forced her to look at me, but she pushed her eyes everywhere else but to mine.

"Talk to me," I begged and I heard the crack in my voice. "Emma, you've been my life for the past eight or nine months. You've been there every breathing moment. Tell me what's going on with you." I swallowed the lump in my throat. "Please."

When her eyes finally settled down, she blinked once, twice and then harder and more frequently as the tears dripped down her face like a faucet.

At last, she spoke. "Why?"

I knew what she meant and the question felt like an icepick being plunged deep into my chest.

"Why did you let last night happen?" she asked, the tears still coming on strong. "It fucks everything up, Morgan." She made a fist and for a beat I feared she might hit me. She didn't.

I reached out and pulled her into my arms, holding her like she had held me after my heartbreaking meeting with E. Richard Kindall's intern. I owed Emma this much, at least.

"What we did was wrong," she said.

I rubbed her back. "What we did was love."

"I won't leave him." She didn't want the failure, I knew that. If Walter left her, she might even fight for him to stay because the prospect of having another failed marriage on her relationship résumé appalled Emma. She wasn't a quitter, she was a fighter. Like Olivia.

I kept holding her. "He doesn't love you like you deserve." But the truth was: "He doesn't love you like I do."

She shook her head, no.

She stepped out of my arms and looked straight at me. "You said you don't believe in love, Morgan. What am I supposed to do with that?"

With my serious-as-a-motherfucker face, I told her: "Leave him."

"No."

I gave her confused-as-a-motherfucker next. "What am *I* supposed to do with *that?*"

"Let go," she told me, and the waterworks started again.

Now it was time for pissed-as-a-motherfucker. "Never. I'm never letting go of you. I can't. I live and breathe and exist and… and live everything Emma. You're my soulmate!"

She grinned, but it was a sad one. "You already said 'live,' Morgan. And you have to let go. You don't have a choice. Because I'm married and I'm not leaving and you live out here and I live out there and this can't happen for us. Not now. Maybe not... ever."

Still pissed-as-a-motherfucker as her face glowed from the endless tears. "That's bullshit, Emma. You love me and I love you. We can't control that. But this distance? *That's* something we can control. We can control it."

She had sadistic written on her face. "Then move."

"I can't! If I *leave* Evelyn, I *lose* Evelyn! Girls need their fathers!" Because I was so angry at the prospect of losing the only woman that ever mattered to me, I hadn't thought my words through. "But you should and can leave, Emma."

She shook her head and heaved a deep breath. "No. I'm married. And my daughters deserve to be close to their fathers just like yours does."

Damn.

We had something of a staring contest next. There was nothing left to argue, nothing much left to say except-

"Goodbye, Morgan. I'm sorry."

And with that, she turned her back on me and walked away, leaving me standing outside the bathrooms like a moron who couldn't stop crying.

CHAPTER THIRTY-ONE

The cab stopped at the curb outside of Rochelle and Sandy's McMansion. I handed the driver a wad of cash, then got out. I didn't make it too far up the driveway when I heard him yell at me.

"You owe me another sixteen bucks, bro," he said.

I reached into my pocket and tossed him another bill, a twenty.

Really, nothing was going the way it was supposed to today. Fucking fuck.

And about halfway to the house, it started pouring. Yeah, the only thing that would make this day worse would have been getting struck by lightning... but then again, maybe that would have alleviated some of this bullshit pain.

At the big wooden door, I hit the doorbell. Once, twice, three times. I heard someone walking on the other side, a little quicker than I expected actually. When the door opened, the hospitable smile that always occupied Rochelle's face melted away and she placed her half-empty wine glass on the floor.

"Oh, honey," she said in that angelic voice of hers and opened her arms to me. "What the hell happened to you?"

★ ★ ★

I told Rochelle everything, starting with last week's marriage counseling session where I arrived at the realization that my marriage would never work itself out, all the way to last night's moment of passion with Emma. And then this morning's moment of heartbreak.

"She's married," I said, shaking my head. "What was I thinking?"

Rochelle had listened patiently this entire time, holding my hands and encouraging me to go on when it felt impossible for me to speak, to breathe. But after that last statement, something changed in her. "You were motivated by your love, honey. Don't beat yourself up. She's the married one, she should have known better."

Her words sucker-punched me. "I never said anything about love," I clarified, even though I remembered somewhat very clearly that I had told Emma I loved her. I gulped. "I just wanted to fuck her, to be with her. I don't believe in that love bullshit anyway."

Rochelle laughed and let go of my hand. "Honey… please."

I didn't like being mocked like this; I was a best-selling author and by now my editor was probably commenting on the absolute, motherfucking genius of *Our Story*. Shouldn't Rochelle be paying me a little more respect? Once *Our Story* broke out, I might be her neighbor and if she didn't want me crashing her pool parties, she had better change her tone.

"Look at you, Morgan," she said, her voice sympathetic again. "You're a wreck. You left your book signing or whatever it is early because of a conversation you had with Emma."

I shrugged. "I don't love her, though."

"Of course you don't," she said, smirking and doing a shitty job trying to hide it. "Yet everything you've done since meeting Emma has been for…?"

I was quiet, listening. I noticed Sandy walking down the hall, checking in on us. Not that he expected that I would try to work my magic on his wife, but he seemed genuinely concerned for me as well; he had seen how well Emma and I clicked. That night at his party had changed things in me, and had even changed things in "us," in

Emma and me.

"She was everything Jennifer never was," Rochelle continued. "Look at how she stroked your ego. She made you feel special. She read your first novel and sent you a pair of her panties. And I'm willing to bet she was the female lead character in this latest story of yours."

Fuck. This was getting uncomfortable because I couldn't believe how well Rochelle could read me. I shifted. Damn. The entire story was Emma – Oliver, Olivia, the heartbreak, the love. Could Rochelle be right? Did I really "love" Emma?

I reminded her of Natalia: "She was the sweetest thing with two legs and that smile of hers turned me on so much that I had to think of old ladies. Without their dentures." And then I brought up Dawn: "If Emma hadn't shown up, I had a box condoms that we would have burned through last night. We were the outcasts of the event, we had so much in common, and she was exactly what I needed – hot, unattached sex. No love, no way; you're wrong about Emma."

Rochelle giggled, checking the time on her wrist. "Then why have you been pouring your heart out for the past two hours, honey?"

Two hours, huh? If I had stuck around the Washington Romance Authors Event, Natalia would have been walking around and telling us to start tidying up. The event would be coming to a close. I wondered what would happen to all of the stuff Emma had purchased for me as a way to help me out because I was pathetic and broke and couldn't look after my own lame ass.

"So what will you do, Morgan?" Rochelle asked me. "Does Emma love you like you love her?"

I thought about that question. I wanted to believe, more than anything, more than I believed in reality, that Emma loved me. But the truth was that no matter how I defined love – my way in terms of love being a habit and routine that could be controlled, or everyone else's way in terms of love being a "heart" condition involving feelings and a spiritual attachment that couldn't be controlled – Emma did not love me. So I shook my head, slowly. It was pretty fucking disappointing to admit that Princess Bitch hadn't loved me and she had been living with me and had a child with me; even more disappointing that someone like Emma with a shit-show record at relationships, an undisputable physical and social attraction to me couldn't love me either. What did that mean for me? Would I die alone?

"She's married," I said. "She won't leave him, no matter how shitty he is to her. And what she said to me today… her ability to just walk away so easily…" I shook my head, then made eye contact with Rochelle. "No, she doesn't love me. She never did."

Rochelle stared back into my eyes, silent.

"As for what I'm going to do, I'm going to disappear. I'm going to rip myself from the habit and routine of Emma."

The way her face crunched and her eyebrows furrowed, I could tell Rochelle was curious.

"I'll start by selling the house. Because for the past however many months, every moment in my empty house was spent fantasizing about Emma."

I hadn't noticed Sandy standing in the corner of the room, leaning against the wall with his arms crossed while he listened in. I would not have been aware at all if he hadn't cleared his throat and asked: "What about your novel? Will you publish it?"

I nodded. "I think I should. I spent a lot of time and brain power on that thing." Not to mention I had no other source of income for the time being.

Rochelle knew where her husband was headed with his question. "But you wrote it as a way to win your wife back. And really, you essentially wrote it with Emma as your template, your benchmark, your guide."

Good point.

"Then what do I do?" I asked. The equity from the house sale would only last so long, and then what?

"Come work with me," Sandy said, pushing away from the wall. "You'll start off at a good salary, we'll put you to good use and it will only help to further rip you out of that habit and routine you keep babbling about."

It sounded good, but Rochelle cautioned: "Are you sure you want to do this, Morgan?"

I didn't have to think long about the aching in my chest, the pain I felt during the entire drive home from the Washington Romance Authors Event. I had made more enemies in this single weekend than I had in my entire life. If I stopped and thought about it, *Our Story* wouldn't have much of a chance once that bestselling twit damaged my reputation among the bloggersphere.

Yes, I needed to move on. I needed to let go. I needed to not only forget about Emma, but create new habits and routines that would make me feel like she never existed.

I looked up at their watchful eyes and nodded. "Yes. I'm sure. This is what I need."

It felt like a fucking intervention.

CHAPTER THIRTY-TWO

Now that there was an end in sight to my marriage, I decided to keep the peace with Princess Bitch. I was completely fine with establishing a new life without her and I knew I could be an adult about this.

The following weekend, I connected with Pretty Boy Jim during Evelyn's drop off.

"Your daughter really hates the Porsche," Pretty Boy Jim confided in me. "What did you say to her? That thing's quicker than a Vette. Now I think I'll have to get rid of it." He leaned closer. "Jenny's not a fan anyway."

I chuckled. "Listen, Jim. You seem to be a good guy."

I changed my mind when he said: "I am actually."

"Anyway, you mentioned your real estate broker friend…"

That put a smile on his face. He patted me on the back despite Princess Bitch yelling at Pretty Boy Jim to hurry up, they were going to be late.

"I'll text you his deets, bro," Pretty Boy said. For the first time since meeting him, I wondered how old he really was… and what he did for a living. Shit.

Once they left, I walked deeper into the house and found Evelyn at the television, her tongue hanging out the corner of her mouth as she concentrated, practicing her gameplay on the Wii. She asked me if I wanted to join, but I said no. We had plans.

"What?" she asked.

Before I could answer, my iPhone vibrated and it seemed odd to me that Pretty Boy Jim would have texted me his real estate broker's details so quickly. But when I checked the screen, all I saw was:

}i{

Emma.

The image forced me to sit down on the sofa. I felt the heat rising in my cheeks and a new, constant throbbing at the base of my skull.

I missed Emma. I missed her so much I hadn't been able to sleep more than 3 hours at once. This absence, this inability to connect with her after we had, well, "connected" last weekend, was killing me. But recognizing my weakness also meant understanding myself a little better. It meant acknowledging that my reconciliation attempts with Jennifer had been more about avoiding the "love" I had developed for Emma than truly wanting to suffer in a hateful marriage for the rest of my life.

"Daddy? Are you going to play, or what?"

I looked at the message one more time before pocketing the phone and picking up the other Wii remote to play a game with my daughter.

Fuck the plans.

★ ★ ★

I took Evelyn out for lunch. Yes, McDonald's because it was cheap, she loved it and I needed to soften her up for the news I was about to tell her. While we ate, I kept checking my iPhone to see if Emma had written again or if she had tried to contact me. The rule had always been that we would send the }i{ and until there was a response, we would lie low, assuming the other would respond when it was safe to do so.

For the most part, it was always safe at my end; less so for Emma who had to deal with a husband who didn't notice her, but might start inquiring if he found her busily texting me while hanging out with him. And then, with time, it became something of a signal. I'd send her the }i{ and she'd send me a nudie pic. Or she'd send me a }i{ and I'd know she was thinking about me.

Today's }i{ could mean anything, but at least I knew she was thinking about me and I figured she probably wanted to call a truce or have a chat or who knows what.

"Daddy?" Evelyn said, her cheeks bulging from the crappy food. "You're destroyed today."

"I am?" I asked. I knew kids were perceptive, but holy shit…

"What are you thinking about?" she asked and I swore she sounded exactly like Dr. Simms.

When I realized that she meant to say *distracted* instead of *destroyed*, I chuckled. So I told her the truth. "I'm starting a new job. Not this Monday, but the next one. And, well, I want to show you where I'll be living."

She frowned at me. Damn, my daughter was smart. Scary smart. "You're moving?"

I put a big smile on my face. "Yes. You'll love how big your room is and it's in a building, which means we get to ride elevators and we can go swimming whenever we want!"

Her eyes lit up.

"Do you want to see it?"

She nodded, spitting out her food in a big blob of gross. "Let's go now."

✯ ✯ ✯

By dinner, Pretty Boy Jim had sent me the phone number that belonged to his real estate broker friend. I called him and he promised to swing by the house tomorrow morning with a contract, comparable sales figures and a For Sale sign that he would hammer into my front yard. He said he knew the area well and alluded to the fact that most of his affluent clients were looking in this area for their children. Without giving a guarantee, he said the house would sell within weeks. Great.

Oh, and Emma had texted once again, too. This time she didn't care if was safe to proceed; she wrote the following message, which made me cry in the bathroom, which was where I had to read it without worrying about Evelyn interrupting me:

Emma: I'm sorry. I'm sorry I hurt you, I'm sorry I let Saturday happen, I'm sorry I love you. I'm sorry I meant every word I ever said, texted, and wrote to you. I'm sorry I will always love you. I'm sorry that because I love you, I have to let you go. I'm sorry our stars aren't aligning. I'm sorry I don't know what the future holds for us and that I will not leave Walter because I'm sorry my vows mean something to me. I'm sorry I can't screw up a second marriage. I'm sorry I can't move out and be with you right now. I'm sorry I sent you that fan mail and I'm sorry that once I got my claws into you I refused to let you go. I'm sorry that you hate me and will never forgive me for what I've done. I'm sorry your life will give you all the happiness you've ever wanted and I'm mostly sorry that I can't be a part of it.

And then, as I finished reading that long text and wiped my eyes clear, she sent another one.

Emma: Morgan, I'm also sorry that this is goodbye.

I reread her sorry message over and over and once my face dried up, I left the phone on the bathroom sink. Upstairs, I found Evelyn waiting for me in her bed, reading a book. Seeing her made me proud; seeing that she was too tall for her toddler bed did not.

"Once we move, you'll have a big bed," I promised. Not only because she needed one, but because her Barbie racecar bed reminded me of the weekend that Emma had spent here, our time at Rochelle and Sandy's, that moment at the Outlook, that first kiss just down the hall. Part of breaking out of the habit and routine of loving

Emma meant I had to get rid of the toddler bed and everything else that reminded me of her.

She smiled, folded her book away and pulled her sheets over her little body. "I love you, Daddy."

I kissed her forehead. "Do you want to play the song game to help you fall asleep?"

She hesitated before saying: "No thanks. You look tired. Good night."

After turning out the lights in her room, I went straight to my bedroom and slipped under the sheets. As had been the tradition since last weekend, I had a tough time falling asleep and at midnight I heard Evelyn's little footsteps creeping into my bedroom. I half-expected her to puke the McDonald's up, but instead she climbed onto my bed, wiggled under the covers and cuddled up to me from behind.

She pretended to be the big spoon, and she held me like she knew I was hurting and wanted to squeeze that pain out of me.

I loved my daughter.

I fell asleep soon thereafter.

✷ ✷ ✷

The smile on Princess Bitch's face the following night when she and Pretty Boy Jim stopped in to pick up Evelyn made me happy. Unable to remember the last time I had been responsible for a smile like that, I stared out the front window at the For Sale sign pegged into the lawn. I felt good about myself. For the first time since moving here, I literally felt happy. Two months ago, my resistance to selling the house had seemed insurmountable, yet here I stood, staring at the front lawn while my wife and the man she was fucking helped themselves to wine in the kitchen.

"Until it sells, I'm still entitled to half of this shit," Princess Bitch barked from the kitchen. I could almost hear the wine pouring into her glass.

Moving away from the relieving sight on the front lawn, I joined them. I grabbed a clean glass and sat at the table. Pretty Boy Jim wasn't drinking and when I asked him why, he shrugged and said he had to drive.

"He's a pussy," Princess Bitch said, raising her cup. Unlike when she insulted me, she used a soft and gentle voice when poking fun at Pretty Boy.

"It's not my place to be here," Pretty Boy elaborated, then finally seemed to relax a little. When he turned to me, he asked: "Did Ronny hook you up? I told him to reduce his commission and call everyone on his list who owes him a favor."

I frowned, sipping some wine. Ronny's lower-than-expected commission had surprised me, but I hadn't mentioned anything to him. Ronny Bovaird was the city's hottest real estate agent, complete with bus and bench advertising and corny television commercials that seemed better suited to a pawn shop or car dealership. I had wondered how Pretty Boy Jim could get Ronny out to my place on Sunday morning, but now I had my answer.

"Will you be buying your next place with Ronny?" Pretty Boy asked.

Before I could answer, I felt my iPhone vibrating in my pocket. It wasn't the two, short vibrations that indicated an incoming text message; they were the long vibrations of an incoming call. I excused myself and, stepping outside for privacy, I checked the call display.

212-555-1234

I recognized the number as Emma's — for the past however many months, I had seen that number on my phone's screen at least half a dozen times every day. Why was she calling me now after saying goodbye last night in her lengthy "sorry" text? I didn't answer, didn't have the energy to swipe my finger across the screen.

I realized I might never escape her, no matter how hard either of us tried.

When Emma gave up and the phone stopped vibrating, I started to pocket the phone and head back into the house when I felt the two short vibrations of an incoming text. I decided to humor myself and see how urgently she needed to reach me (I wasn't expecting any urgency at all but a part of me, deep *deep* down, hoped that she had realized that she couldn't survive without me and was calling and texting to say she was going to leave Walter after all and was moving closer).

Instead, I saw a short, curt and possibly even hurt message:

Emma: You're not wasting any time getting rid of me, are you?

Rolling my eyes, I headed back into the house. Despite the tremendous weight on my chest from having to ignore Emma, it dawned on me that I was opting to spend my time with Princess Bitch and Pretty Boy Jim instead of sending a response to Emma. By most counts, life was suddenly super-fucked up.

On Tuesday afternoon when I entered Dr. Simms's office, he looked up from a pile of documents at the reception desk and nearly fell over. Princess Bitch had picked me up for this session and seeing us walk in together, on time, was clearly a shock to our marriage counselor.

"Well, well," he said. "Come in."

If Dr. Simms had thought, even for one second, that Princess Bitch and I had arrived together because we had figured out a way to fall back in love, he was dead wrong. And our amicable state pretty much ended with the carpooling because Princess Bitch settled into the sofa across from mine, just like she normally would.

"I have to say," he started, "I was both surprised and impressed to see you arriving together." Then, to me because I had missed last week's session: "How are you feeling, Morgan?"

I gave him a nod, then glanced at Princess Bitch to see if she wanted to tell him the good news or if she wanted me to. When she nodded at me, I cleared my throat. "Jennifer and I have decided to move forward with divorce."

I wasn't quite sure what to expect from Dr. Simms. But he gave an understanding nod that struck me as somewhat contradictory.

Jennifer pitched in: "We'll figure 'us' out in the big picture of things, but 'us' as a couple just isn't right. For either of us."

I agreed. "We both deserve happiness. I didn't represent that for her, and she didn't represent it for me. But we have a daughter-"

"The sweetest daughter anyone could ask for," Princess Bitch corrected.

"And because of her, we'll figure this out."

Dr. Simms crossed his legs at the knees and considered our confession. "When you first came to me, you were both extremely resentful. Now you seem to get along. Not just as two adults should, but as two friends. Tell me what's changed. We'll start with you, Morgan."

I told him that when Jennifer and I were married, I expected my world would begin and end with her. Next to Dr. Simms, Jennifer made a gagging sound, which he asked her to stop doing because it was disruptive.

"But life happens and things change," I said. "Life changed us. Maybe it wasn't so much a change as it was a realization that there was something missing in our relationship." I glanced at Princess Bitch to try and decipher how volatile she was today, then refocused my attention on Dr. Simms when I realized it didn't matter; I was safe. Well, as safe as one could get in a room with Princess Bitch. "With Jennifer, I lacked the love I needed. All I wanted was someone to pay attention to me. I know it sounds girly, but it's the truth. She never paid any attention to me or what I wanted, and that killed me."

"Bullshit," she said. And because she wasn't yelling or throwing herself at me, I could tell she knew it was the truth.

"When I worked for Gervais and Porter," I elaborated, "I was promoted two times. You never asked, not once, how work was going. I never told you about those promotions because you just didn't care."

Jennifer reached into her purse for her iPhone, so I continued with Dr. Simms. "I also wanted someone who could just love me. And convince me that she loved me. Not only did Jennifer never tell me she loved me, but even if she tried, I would never have believed her. Ours was a broken relationship from the start, but I never realized it. So when she walked out, I hated her. I wanted her back because people don't just 'walk out.' People fight for love. They fight for survival."

"We didn't have any love to fight for," Princess Bitch muttered.

"You're right," I agreed. "But we had routine and habit. When you left, my routines and habits felt incomplete. I wanted you back so I could fill those gaps, those empty spots in my day, in everything I did."

Dr. Simms's pensive face told me he was listening. But he also had questions. "Is that really how you feel about love, Morgan? Like it's something that can fill 'gaps' in your daily routine and habits?"

I gave it some thought – nah, I just *pretended* to think about it because his question had been haunting me since Emma crushed my soul – and then nodded. I knew the answer and if Dr. Simms believed "love" existed, good for him; he charged $350/hour to talk about that bullshit, which meant he made a lot more money than I did. But it didn't mean he was right.

He let out a disappointed, "hmm," then faced Princess Bitch. She tucked her phone away. "What about you, Jennifer? What do you believe about love?"

Oddly, she consulted me before she spoke. "You might not like any of this. So I'm sorry."

I rolled my eyes. "Nothing you say can be worse than the twelve years you robbed from me."

"Fuck you, Morgan."

I blew her a kiss, and that ended our sidebar conversation. She faced Dr. Simms and said, "It's James. Period. All that touchy-feely bullshit Morgan talks about? It's James. Everything from the way he fucks me to the money he brings home to the things he buys me and Evelyn, James is Love. With a capital L. He makes me feel things I have never felt before. He was raised by a single mother, just like I was. He loves being outdoors, loves hiking and doing things that keep you healthy. And I love doing shit like that too. James and I, when we talk about 'us,' we talk about our future. We agree or disagree on certain parts, but we talk about it and we decide to head down that path. Together." She let out a long sigh. "With Morgan, if we didn't agree, we proceeded down those paths separately, or we didn't head down them at all. There was never an agreement or compromise and often there was never even a plan."

"I hate structure," I mumbled, wondering for the millionth time how I expected to survive working with Sandy at his high-tech company next week.

"Sometimes," Princess Bitch said, "you sacrifice individual things in order to achieve something for a greater purpose. James cares about everything that involves me and him and Evelyn, it's never about his selfish needs. He's adaptable."

Dr. Simms stepped in at that point. "So with James, he meets a relatively exhaustive list of criteria you need to have met in order for you to feel loved? And to give love in return?"

Princess Bitch agreed with a nod. "Yes. For the most part, I can tick all of the boxes on that checklist, if that's what you're asking. I mean, it's not perfect – nothing's perfect – but he's there. He meets all of the important requirements."

Dr. Simms let out a long breath. "Nothing's perfect, huh?"

I really didn't care if Dr. Simms wanted to tear a piece out of Princess Bitch's ego, but she was right. I knew I had a checklist of my own. For example, when I first met Emma, her failed marriages, her teenage-pregnancy, her promiscuity, all of that fit into my checklist. So I agreed that nothing was perfect, but if you could check enough boxes on that checklist, it was as close to perfect as you could expect to get. Fuck, again look at Emma. For me, she was as close to perfect as I would ever find, yet from an objective distance she was so far from perfect it made me sick to my stomach.

"With all due respect," I chirped. "Perfection is bullshit. Jennifer is right, it doesn't exist."

I could see that Dr. Simms didn't agree with our view, but he also knew better than to confront us. Two against one. Plus I had the benefit of Princess Bitch being on *my* team for once. He was outmuscled here, so he let it go.

We chatted a little more and Dr. Simms suggested we meet once per month for the next six months. Just to see how things were going and to stay focused on our friendship. Jennifer and I exchanged glances, but we ultimately agreed to the monthly sessions. I personally didn't think we needed them, but what he hell; if nothing else, maybe Jennifer and I could reform this deranged love-believing motherfucker who sounded like a Fischer-Price character into a human being who recognized how relationships worked in the real world.

"Well," Dr. Simms said, "I'm happy to see you've come to an agreement. But I'll add this, and maybe it's something to think about until we meet again in a month's time. I believe that love is perfect. I believe that there's no checklist. In fact, I believe in the imperfection of people, but that it's love that allows us to see so far beyond those blemishes that they do not exist to our eyes."

I immediately thought of that dried up, sun-damaged receptionist of a wife that Dr. Simms had… if he seriously considered her to be perfect, then maybe he had a valid point.

"I believe that once you start to quantify love by measuring your mates on a checklist, you're trying to convince yourself of something that isn't there. Because you can't quantify love. You can quantify students, employees, things you own or want to own, but you can't quantify something that makes you see beyond the very same things you're measuring."

Damn, he was good – whatever the fuck he was trying to say. But it struck me as awfully convenient that his genius of $350/hour was only coming to the surface today. Where had this bullshit been up until now?

"With that in mind, let's try to look beyond the checklists. And Morgan, once you change your routine and habits, know that love will still be there if it's true love. You'll only forget if it's not the real thing. Because when it's true love, you can't hide anywhere, you can't disappear behind new stuff and new jobs and new interests. True love will follow you wherever you go." He shrugged. "Again, that's just what I believe."

He stood up and indicated that our marriage counseling session had come to an end.

CHAPTER THIRTY-THREE

The following Tuesday night, Princess Bitch hurried over to the house. Alone. She was to meet me here to sign papers for Ronny. There were multiple offers on our property and he needed us together to sift through them and pick a winner. Jennifer arrived before Ronny, and when I looked past her and asked, "Where's Jim?" she called me an asshole and walked straight to the kitchen.

"Seriously, where is he?"

"He's watching Evelyn, it's her bed-time," Princess Bitch said as she poured herself some wine.

Then she asked me about my new job with Sandy's company, and I talked for fifteen or more minutes, non-stop, about how much I enjoyed it. Even the routine and rigid corporate culture made me happy. "Because it makes me feel important. If I don't show up, if I don't do my job, someone else is fucked and the system breaks down. And every company needs an accounting system for it to operate smoothly and efficiently."

She rolled her eyes and I could tell she wanted to yawn. "What about *Our Story*? When are you going to publish that? I want to be famous."

I felt my iPhone vibrate against my thigh and glanced at the screen:

Emma: I miss my }i{

The text made me chuckle, but I ignored it anyway. I didn't know how she could miss her }i{ … what had happened to it, I wondered? It wasn't something you could lose or misplace. But then again, her definition of }i{ was not the same as mine.

"Morgan? The book?"

I shrugged. "The editor liked it. A lot. But I've just been too busy to make the changes. I don't think I'll publish this one."

She didn't like that, but before she could start insulting me and making me feel worthless, the doorbell rang. I hurried to answer it, welcoming Ronny to the kitchen. He passed on a glass of wine but presented the different offers, saving the best for last.

"Now this one," he said, pulling it out like it was the Holy Grail. "It's firm. If you sign this one, your house is sold and you're moving into a new place in less than a month. Keep in mind, it's ten thousand dollars below the highest offer and only five grand below your asking price. But it's firm and these buyers are serious. They've given a twenty-thousand dollar deposit, well above what anyone else offered."

Princess Bitch and I exchanged just one glance before turning to Ronny and saying, "Sold!"

★ ★ ★

Change happens fast, sometimes at the snap of your fingers, like when you forget to look both ways before crossing the street and step in front of a speeding transport truck. And just like that, life's landscape changes and it never looks the same again because you're dead or you're clinging to life by your fingernails.

For me, that type of radical change didn't happen so quickly, but it felt just as painful. Within three weeks, I had moved out of the first and only house I had ever owned, the only house my daughter had ever known, the one place I had felt most comfortable and at peace. In that same period of time, we filed our divorce papers and I returned to the grind of full-time employment. Interestingly, working with someone that I respected and admired (Sandy) made the daily routine of a worker-bee much less agonizing.

That man amazed me, and not only because he drove a Vette on weekends and had married Rochelle. I watched him with a Brokeback kind of awe because when it came to numbers, Sandy had the same type of skill that I possessed when it came to words. He pulled the most beautiful financial solutions seemingly out of thin air. Then he would host a meeting with his entire team to discuss his solution and by the end of any given day, Sandy's art became a filtered-down ledger entry (or fifty in the case of our company's latest venture into Iceland).

On the rare occasion, like today, where he booked lunch with me to discuss the technical matters surrounding our corporate projects, I was certain that the others in his department figured we were having a closet affair. If anyone dared to ask me if I loved this man, I would admit that I did – in many ways, Sandy had saved my life and turned it around; those are the types of people you tend to love indefinitely.

"What kind of progress have you made with the college

regarding your transcripts?" Sandy asked, stuffing a sandwich into his mouth.

"They've apparently sent it by registered mail," I said. "To the office because no one can sign for it at the condo during the day."

He nodded. Sandy didn't fuck around during the workweek. He was 100% business. Next, he asked me about the progress I was making with our Finance group on a rate swap we needed to execute in the coming weeks. "Who's really holding this up, the bank or Finance?"

I gave him my opinion of Finance and admitted that I had spoken with our bank and not only did the bankers know what they were doing, but they seemed more than willing to meet our request. "The bankers are easygoing and want the commission, they want this done. But you know Finance."

He chuckled. "Special breed, aren't they?"

"They sure are."

We spoke a little bit more about other work projects, but we soon left the deli and were back at work. Twenty-minute lunches with the CFO didn't bother me – it bothered everyone else in the office, though.

And I loved it. I loved every minute of my nine-to-fiver. Already three months into this gig and I hadn't even used any of my sick days or vacation entitlement.

✶ ✶ ✶

My new condo had great views of downtown. From my sofa in the living room, I could watch the lights in the corporate towers flicker off around 8:00pm when the most-dedicated (or incompetent, depending on your point of view) employees left for the night, then back on around eleven when the cleaning staff arrived to tidy up. If I walked onto the balcony, I could breathe in the crisp, late-Fall air and watch the traffic below – quiet throughout the week, but busier on a Friday night.

Since I didn't have Evelyn this weekend, I poured myself a whiskey on the rocks, and watched a new release on Netflix – it seemed to be my new routine these days. By eleven o'clock, I passed out from the booze and boredom, and the next morning I woke up energized.

I went straight to my desk. I checked my bank accounts (happy to see that I had a shit load of cash from the sale of house – not so happy that I didn't have time to spend it) and email inboxes. Inevitably, I came across *Our Story*, which I sometimes read during quiet weekends like this one for shits and gigs. I enjoyed the story and a lot of *Sextual Encounters* fans kept bugging me about when my next masterpiece would get released. A few of them knew about the Washington Romance Writers Event fiasco, but most of them seemed to chalk it up as nothing more than a rumor – after all, Emma was beautiful and I was not.

When I checked my sinking *Sextual Encounters* rankings on Amazon, I also checked on Emma's and discovered that hers were following the same downward spiral into oblivion as mine. Neither of us was killing it as authors at the moment.

Staring at my computer monitor, I decided that I would not allow Emma to ruin this story for the rest of my audience. I uploaded the appropriate files, I set my price and let the cursor hover over the *Publish* button. I always seemed to have second thoughts at this particular moment. And as always, I decided to think on it a little more before publishing.

Pussy.

I closed the computer screen and stepped away.

I hated Emma at moments like this. Hated that she had engrained herself into so much of me that I couldn't even make a decision about a book – another brilliant one, no doubt – that I had written and couldn't publish because I refused to let her think that I was –

My phone vibrated in my pocket and glancing at the screen I saw the symbol:

}i{

I hadn't heard from her in over two months, maybe even three (okay, it was exactly 77 days). Why was she bugging me all of a sudden? She had clearly put an end to our relationship. It hurt to think that I was dumped by someone I had only seen two or three times – I hadn't even had a real opportunity to fuck things up with her; at least with Princess Bitch, I had made her life frustrating and depressing for twelve years. Jennifer had a reason to want nothing to do with me; Emma didn't.

I ignored the text message and decided it was time to change my phone number. It was the only solution to completely ridding myself of this heartache that even the change in habit and routine couldn't soften. So I hopped in the shower, got changed and even though I now owned a car (nothing fancy, just a small Honda Civic that spent more time in my underground parking garage than on the streets) decided to walk to the nearest AT&T store downtown.

Not even a block from the condo, I heard the footsteps running up behind me. I stepped to the side of the sidewalk so the jogger could pass me, but those footfalls slowed and before I knew it, the person was walking right beside me. The faint breeze brought that familiar lemon-cream scent to my nostrils and I knew, without having to look over at her, that it was Emma.

She pretended to not notice me, fake-texting on her iPhone as an alibi. But I knew that was bullshit because what were the chances of Emma going for a jog and ending up right beside me, in my city thousands of miles away from hers? Regardless, I refused to play her stupid games and kept my focus on the ground, pretending that I hadn't noticed her either. We were two adults acting like preschoolers.

We continued like that for a full city block, just the two of us walking these streets on a Saturday morning at ten o'clock.

At last, she stomped her feet, grabbed my arm and forced me to stop and look at her.

"Morgan…" she said. She wore a smile on her lips, one that was sad and hopeful at the same time. "You can't ignore me forever."

I stared back into her eyes for the longest minute or so of my life. It hurt to see her, to feel her soft touch on my arm like that, to smell that lemon-cream filling wafting off her in the soft breeze. I was ruined, she had done this to me, and yet she was the only person who could fix me.

"Please talk to me," she said, practically begging me. "I came all this way."

I didn't know if I could do it because my throat was tight and it hurt and I could barely breathe, but I managed to ask a single question anyway. "How did you find me?"

She chuckled, but I could tell she wasn't too proud of her investigative work. "I started at the house. I knew where that was – I had the address, remember? When the new owners answered, I asked if they knew where you were but they obviously didn't. So I asked what real estate agent represented them in the purchase. That was two days ago."

"Their agent told you were to find me?"

"No, he told me where to find *your* real estate agent."

"And then?" What the hell happened to personal privacy?

"Your agent was professional outside of asking me out on a date, which I refused. Obviously that was the wrong response because then he clammed up and wouldn't tell me anything at all."

"Then how?" I asked. If I remembered correctly, that had been my original question.

"His assistant. I went to their office again yesterday, when I knew Ronny wouldn't be there, and showed her some of your naked pictures."

"What?!?"

She laughed. "Don't worry, I covered up your private parts, but she obviously recognized you and knew who you were. 'The so-called brilliant writer,' was how she referred to you."

What?! I wasn't a mere "writer," I was a fucking "author." I hated how people used those words like they were synonymous.

"And then, well," Emma continued, but now she glanced down at her feet because this was the part she wasn't too proud about. "I showed her pictures of my daughter, an old one from when she was born – it's the wallpaper on my iPhone, so it was handy. I told her that you were the father and you deserved to know this."

Okay, *that* part was pretty clever. "It was that easy, huh?"

Emma shrugged, looking up with subtle pride touching her lips. "That's not exactly easy, Morgan. But lucky for me, the assistant was a single mother just like I was when I was in my early twenties. So we got talking about the difference between guys who man up and face their issues, and those that completely fall off the grid. No, not 'fall off' but *jump* off the grid."

"But I'm not your daughter's father," I told her. "And I didn't jump off the grid. I gave you exactly what you wanted, which was space to make your relationship work." I swallowed the groan that begged to escape. "You're welcome for that, by the way."

She studied me with the same big, beautiful eyes that had me falling in love with her in the first place. "You think you know what I want, do you?"

"Only what you've told me, Emma."

Her faced scrunched into a ball of confusion. "Words don't mean anything to writers like us, remember? So why do you place so much emphasis on them?"

"Words are the only things we've got when it comes to communicating," I argued. "If you tell me to leave you alone because you won't move or get rid of your husband who doesn't know you exist, what else am I supposed to believe?"

She stepped closer to me and I realized that she was still holding my wrist. She brought my hand to her chest, asked me to listen to what our hearts said, not what our mouths said.

I pulled my hand away because even though I loved the sensation that her fake breasts left on my palm, I knew where touching them would lead us and it had taken me all of this time to survive the aftermath from the last time that had happened.

"I did listen to your tits," I said, realizing after the words left my mouth that I meant to say *heart*. "But the next day, you were crying. You regretted that night, that one and only night we ever had together." I shook my head and snapped back to reality. "Emma, what are you doing here, why are you doing this?"

Her eyes darted across my face. It took her a moment to find the right "meaningless" words, but they eventually came once her Attention Deficit Disorder settled. "This isn't perfect, Morgan. I can appreciate that and I don't like it any more than you do. But I've tried what you're doing, what you've done. I've tried forgetting about you, moving on and rediscovering my life as a way to replace those moments where the only things that mattered before was your texts, pictures and phone calls. I tried so hard and even though I had days where I succeeded in not thinking about you at all, all I could think about was… was you. And how I wasn't thinking of you, but really I was." She showed me her hands. "I can't even look at my own hands without thinking about you. I've touched myself with these hands and in those moments of intense self-love, it was your face that I saw hovering over mine."

I caught myself nodding because I knew exactly what she was experiencing; I remembered those nights of stroking myself to the image of Emma on top of me, rolling her hips as I fucked her the many ways she had promised we would fuck each other. So yes, I knew her pain because in the morning when I lay awake before getting ready for work, those moments on my back were the worst. The flood of memories not only killed my motivation, but they reminded me of a perfection I could never have all to myself.

"I never believed in this kind of thing," she said, motioning between us. "My girlfriends who got dumped and never got over the breakup – even to this day, some of them still remember that first true love – were pathetic, at least to me. I never understood it. Not until I met you. And now I'm acquainted really well with that kind of emotion. I'm familiar with how time can pass where you pine and wait and pray, all of it in complete and utter denial. And all you think about is that other person, even though he will never come back." Her eyes filled with tears and it broke my heart to see the pain in them. "Like you're not coming back, are you?"

"Emma," I started, but she shook her head to interrupt me.

"Can I finish?" she asked, her voice cracking. "I realize that I'm flawed. Walter and I never should have been married. I know that my staying with him, staying in this failure of a marriage doesn't help anyone – it certainly doesn't help you – because you own me, all of me; all he owns is my time right now. But something it proves to everyone, *especially* you, is that I won't give up. On anything." She paused, possibly for dramatic effect because that was what any good actress would do. "And if I promise that I will refuse to ever give up on *us*, Morgan, when our time comes and we're together, how can I just leave him? I can't."

"Emma," I started, but she interrupted me again.

"I'm not wrong about us."

I looked around, reminded that we stood outside, a few short blocks from downtown. If Emma were selling Girl Guide cookies, I would have bought some. But she wasn't, so I wasn't buying.

"Say something," she said.

I breathed, bringing myself back down to earth before finally opening my mouth. "You know something, Emma? I used to have this recurring daydream about you. In it you would show up at my new place. After hunting me down, days of serious stalking – kind of like what you did – you'd catch me off guard, exactly as you have, as I leave my condo for Starbucks to get my morning fix. I'd be just down the street when there you are, seemingly out of nowhere. Again, just like now. And would I stop and take you in, all of you, and when our eyes lock we'd just stare into each other's souls and all of that lost time would come out in the shape of a big smile, a few tears, and a tight hug that feels like… I don't know, it would feel like *home*."

At that, Emma brought her body to mine, wrapped her arms around me and cried softly against my chest. It took me some time to open my own arms to her, but I did. And it felt like home, just like I always knew it would. But I wasn't done speaking yet. I let her finish with the tears because I considered myself a good guy like that, and when it felt safe to do so, I stepped back and memorized everything about her in that specific breath of time.

"But you know, sometimes you outgrow your home. I didn't. In my case, Jennifer moved out for no reason or warning one day, and she took our daughter with her. So essentially my home outgrew me and my budget. And now that I've moved, I'm fucking happier. It might not be perfect, it might not have the white picket fence, and now I've got the D-badge on my marriage record, but I'm wearing it like a badge of honor, not like you. I'm shying away from admitting failure because without my divorce, I wouldn't be here right now, would I?"

"Morgan…"

"It's my turn to finish, Emma," I said. "I loved you for everything. Your successes and intelligence as well as your failures. I loved you just like you said you loved me, but I loved you more. I wrote a novel about you – Oliver, Olivia, it's all you, one hundred percent you."

She looked confused. "You wrote it to win Jennifer back."

I shook my head, no. "I thought so too. Because when I wrote about you and how you made me feel and how our life had all of these obstacles before us and everything else, I thought to myself: Who wouldn't fall in love with this story? But that story is you, Emma. Every word. And I fell in with you."

The tears started again, but when she came to me for a supportive hug, I stepped back. This hurt her; I saw the sting in her eyes. She asked me if I needed to be somewhere.

"No, not me. But you do. You need to go now," I said, nodding.

"I can't go. I love you."

"You were right. At the Washington Romance Authors Event, everything you said was right. I just didn't want to believe it. And now that I'm in a better place, you can't just rob my sanity after I fought so hard to earn it back."

"I don't want to be *right*, Morgan! I just want us to *do* things right!"

"You're married."

She stomped her foot. "I'm dealing with that."

I stared into the distance, wondering how late the wireless store was going to stay open today. When my attention came back to Emma, I saw that I had broken her. And I hated myself for that because I wasn't sure if I would be the one to fix her.

I told her: "I have to get going."

The silence between us seemed to last an eternity. As we stared at each other, her fingers reached toward mine and traced long lines on my hand. We didn't hug, didn't really say anything else until it was goodbye. No happily ever after, not today.

"I wasn't wrong about us," she said, her voice hard and determined. But because there were words attached to that voice of hers, I didn't place a whole lot of trust in them. "Morgan, I love you. No matter what happens, whether you hate me and never speak with me or see me again, I will always love you and the time we shared. And because of this love, I will always be waiting for you, just like Olivia waits until the end of time for Oliver. I'll be there, always waiting, always for you." She smiled at that point, and the sadness and doubt from earlier was gone.

"Goodbye, Emma."

"Bye, Morgan."

We both walked away, going our separate ways – me toward downtown, Emma back toward the condo. But after a few steps, she called my name and I stopped. I didn't look back because I didn't possess the strength I needed to let her go; one look, and I'd become her victim again.

"Don't forget," she yelled.

"Forget what?"

"Don't forget you belong to me," she answered. "In a non-friction kind of way of course."

Although it was impossible for her to see the satisfaction on my face, she surely saw me shaking my head before I continued walking, more committed than ever to changing my phone number and stepping forever out of the reach of Emma's words.

EPILOGUE

April 4th, 2014. It's a late Friday night after a 60-hour workweek with Sandy. I had spent so much of that time making sure our Accounting department was properly optimizing his latest tax-efficiency strategy. I now love numbers more than anything else in this world. Well, everything except for Balzac's, the newest espresso bar that I go out of my way to visit on my way into work every morning.

As with all non-Evelyn weekends, I pour myself a glass of whiskey on the rocks. But this Friday is a little different than the others, so I pour more than my usual dosage. And then I step outside to my patio. Despite the early-April temperatures, it's warmer than seasonal and the nicest it has been since moving into my new house. I have become something an expert mover in the past twelve months, but I figure I will stay here.

I sit on the steps leading from the house to the backyard because I don't own any patio furniture yet – not a whole hell of a lot of real furniture either – and retrieve the Cohiba that one of my coworkers imported for me. It's dark out, the sky is pretty clear with just a few clouds, and when I light the tip of the Cohiba, it's like there's another star in the sky.

The significance of this date will never wear off. For one, it's the anniversary of Olivia Warren and Oliver Weaver's first kiss. It's the night Oliver spends on his own backyard patio and, like me, stares up at the sky. But unlike me, he looks for a shooting star that always comes. In my case, there's no shooting star, but I stare up there anyway.

Because for me it was the day I met Emma.

As for Oliver Weaver…

Saying goodbye has never been easy for Oliver. Whether it was that first goodbye following her visit to Chicago or the goodbye that came after the last time he made love to her and had to return to work (yes, it had been a lunch-hour quickie) Oliver knows he wasn't been built for goodbyes.

He closes his eyes and all he has to do is picture her perfect face.

She's smiling, always smiling and she has the finest white teeth he has ever seen. He reaches out to that face and takes it with his hands and her smile brightens at his touch, like it always does.

"I love you," he whispers to her. "I've known it from the moment we met. It's why I didn't need to make love to you that first night in your hotel room. Because you gave me more than that, you still do and you always will."

"Oliver Weaver," she says through her happy lips, her eyes with that gleam in them again. "Nobody loves me as perfectly as you do."

He always has some difficulty with that statement. Because he regrets never loving her as perfectly as she deserved. Whether earlier on when he remained married to his ex-wife, or right now, when death keeps them apart, he knows his love isn't perfect.

"I'll never stop loving you," he says, and he knows his eyes have a gleam in them too. Except in his eyes, that gleam belongs to the sadness, to the ache of having only this one moment with her, this moment that happens whenever his eyes are closed. This moment that, for most people and their "logical" definitions and laws, doesn't exist.

Olivia gives him a stupid big smile now. It says she believes him like only a soulmate could, and then she presses her lips to his under the moonlight of that April 4th sky.

Their imperfect love is a lot like that John Hancock Center that confused him as a child. Where the taller, more-notorious Sears Tower has a plain black surface, the John Hancock has iron beams that crisscross its length. Their love is a lot like that – crisscrossing the surface of an eclipsed but beautiful life, but never intersecting long enough to make an impact on those that witness it.

"I'm still fighting," she whispers in his ear.

And then she's gone.

Always smiling and always gone.

I refuse to publish *Our Story* even though I have uploaded it a dozen times over the past month alone (not once tonight, though). There are obvious reasons for my refusal and one of them is this: the vibrating phone in my pocket on this special day.

Somehow, some way, Emma knows. She knows everything, and I don't have to look at my jAppe screen to confirm this.

But I look anyway, just like I'll sometimes look at Ariana's cleavage when she bends over at the office, or up Rochelle's skirt when I'm at her house having dinner and she uncrosses her legs to get more comfortable.

What I find on the screen makes me smile. It always does, because it tells me she's still looking for me and wants me to know it:

}i{

THE END

Well…. Sort of.

ACKNOWLEDGEMENTS

This novel never would have been possible without the help and encouragement of a gazillion people, many of whom I will forget to mention – sorry.

All of the bloggers, readers and fans for creating such a huge venue for writers, both independent and traditionally published… for your passion… for your insistence and collective voice when it comes to this new era of storytelling. Without each one of you, this world of ours would not exist. All it takes is one sale… and the next Amanda

Hocking, Hugh Howey or Colleen Hoover is discovered. Thank you for allowing me to play in a corner of your sandbox.

Amy Louise Clark (Clarksy) for having the patience, passion and patience for my story, patience for me in general, and patience for my inability to sit still and/or focus. Did I mention patience? Without you and your lists, I would never have fully understood that social media was meant for more than just flirting with people (in my defense, *most* were women).

Leslie Fear of The Indie Bookshelf and co-author of *Villere House*, for your ongoing support, friendship and insight. You were my first non-relative fan (still no fan mail, mind you) and without you I would have stopped before I ever began.

Cathy Givans for editing and providing the kind of honest feedback and moral support that I needed throughout this project. In those moments when I wanted to cry or die (often both) your comments made me laugh. And cry. Always when I needed ~~to~~ it the most.

Lastly, I would not have written the first word of Non Friction without Rick Marin. If I hadn't met you when I had, I would still be empty, blind and done. You've given me strength beyond words, faith beyond comfort and insight beyond sight. This story exists because of you and what you have taught me and continue to teach me on a daily basis.

About the Author

Morgan Parker is the pen name for a shy and introverted banker. He currently divides his time between Toronto, Canada and his imagination. When he isn't writing or working with clients or relaxing at Balzac's with a medium non-fat cappuccino, Morgan Parker enjoys spending time with his family. And sleeping, preferably on a bed (the left side) but depending on the day, he can pretty much curl up anywhere. No, he is not currently accepting applications for cuddling partners.

He loves interacting with bloggers, readers and fans, and if you consider yourself one of those, you can reach him through his Facebook page. Although he doesn't particularly enjoy interacting with people who yell at him, he is always happy to chat with anyone, especially if their criticism will help with his writing. So next time you're on Facebook, look for Morgan Parker and Like his author page!